SUSAN ROGERS COOPER

A CROOKED LITTLE HOUSE

AN E. J. PUGH MYSTERY

This is a work of fiction. Names, characters, places and incidents either are the product of the author's imagination or are used fictitiously. Any resemblance to actual events, locales, organizations, or persons, living or dead, is entirely coincidental and beyond the intent of either the author or the publisher.

AVON BOOKS, INC.
1350 Avenue of the Americas
New York, New York 10019

Inside cover author photo by Kate Linger
Published by arrangement with the author
Visit our website at **http://www.AvonBooks.com/Twilight**
Library of Congress Catalog Card Number: 98-93311
ISBN: 0-380-79469-1

First Avon Twilight Printing: January 1999

AVON TWILIGHT TRADEMARK REG. U.S. PAT. OFF. AND IN OTHER COUNTRIES, MARCA REGISTRADA, HECHO EN U.S.A.

Printed in the U.S.A.

WCD 10 9 8 7 6 5 4 3 2 1

To my sisters,
in law and love,
Sissy and Karli

Praise for
Edgar nominated author
SUSAN ROGERS COOPER

"One of today's finest mystery writers."
Carolyn Hart, author of *Death in Paradise*

"WELL, I'D SAY YEAH, I THINK SHE'S DEAD."

"I agree with you, Ruthanne," the sheriff said. "About five hours, give or take, don't you think?"

She stood up and hastily removed her gloves. "That sounds about right to me, Sheriff," she said.

I could feel my anger building. Nobody cared. Ruthanne obviously found the whole thing distasteful; and the sheriff was thinking only of how expeditiously he could wrap the whole thing up. Juney lay dead in front of all these people and nobody cared. Would her four-year-old boy be the only one to grieve for her?

Moncrief made a motion with his hand and one of the deputies rolled the body over, face up.

I stared. I moved closer.

It wasn't Juney.

Other E. J. Pugh Mysteries by
Susan Rogers Cooper
from Avon Twilight

ONE, TWO, WHAT DID DADDY DO?
HICKORY DICKORY STALK
HOME AGAIN, HOME AGAIN
THERE WAS A LITTLE GIRL

Acknowledgments

I'd like to thank William Reid, Travis County Assistant District Attorney; Tom Garner, attorney-at-law; Judith Miller, M.S.W.; and Don Cooper for their assistance in the creation of this manuscript. I'd also like to thank my agent Vicky Bijur and my editor Ann McKay Thoroman for their patience and support.

One

Puddin' piddled on Vera's carpet. Megan pulled the cookie jar off the counter and broke it into a thousand pieces. Graham said something obscene to someone on the phone. And Vera, my mother-in-law, talked to me in no uncertain terms with about a dozen straight pins sticking out of her mouth. I had no idea what she said, but assumed it had something to do with either Puddin', Megan, or Graham. So I just looked grim and nodded.

At present I could do nothing about the piddle, the cookie jar, or the obscenity. I was sitting with my legs crossed in the middle of Vera's living-room floor with approximately two tons of tulle spread across my lap. Okay, I exaggerate. But not by much. Eighteen-year-old Brenna, Vera's ward and my friend, was standing on the coffee table with taffeta draped over her cutoffs and T-shirt. Bessie, my third child, stood by the coffee table staring with her mouth open at Brenna, no doubt having fantasies of her own prom to come—in another eleven years.

In order to keep my hand in, I yelled, "Graham, get off the phone!"

This, of course, did as much good as telling Puddin', our one-year-old half-rottweiler half–bassett hound puppy, not to wet on the carpet. "Bessie, go tell Megan to clean up that mess in the kitchen, and don't anybody touch any of those cookies. You'll cut yourselves!"

"Like Megan did when she got that Kiss with the glass in it?" she asked.

I shuddered. "Yeah, just like that. Scoot."

With one last, longing look at Brenna, Bessie took off to the kitchen to do what she does best—sweetly order her siblings around.

Brenna screeched as a pin found its way into her flesh.

"Than thiw," Vera said, or something similar.

"Stand still," I said, taking a wild guess at interpretation.

Graham came in and stood with his hands on his hips, his face indignant. "There was someone on the phone trying to sell Grandma a funeral plot!" he said. "I told them what they could do with that!"

"We all heard," I assured my son. "Make sure the mess in the kitchen is really picked up and thrown away, lay down some paper towels on Puddin's mess, then take the girls, the dogs, and yourself into the backyard."

"Would you like me to rotate the tires in my spare time?" my son said.

"Your sarcasm is lost on me," I said. "I left my sense of humor in my other pants."

"Oo neba aa en oomu," Vera said.

"And whatever she said."

Vera very deliberately took the pins from her mouth. "I said you never had a sense of humor to begin with."

"Go," I told Graham, who reluctantly left, stealing his own last glance at Brenna, the girl of his eleven-year-old dreams.

"Miss Vera," Brenna said, a frown on her pretty face, "are you sure this is gonna look like the pattern?"

"Have I ever steered you wrong, honey?" Vera asked.

"You fixed liver and told me it was beef," she said.

"It *was* beef. Calves liver *is* beef, honey." Vera stuck the pins back in her mouth and her reading glasses back on her nose.

Brenna crinkled her nose, and whispered to me, "It was awful."

"Aug hug da," Vera said.

"She heard that," I interpreted.

The doorbell rang. The kids were in the backyard, Brenna was pinned to the coffee table, and Vera wasn't moving.

"I'll get it," I said, with as much grace as Graham would have under similar circumstances. Which is to say, none at all. I clamored out from under the tons of tulle and got creakily to my feet. My left leg was asleep as I dragged myself to the front door.

A woman and a small boy, about four years old, were standing on Vera's wide front porch. The woman was a scrawny little thing, all elbows and knees, wearing too many layers of clothes for the weather, carrying a beat-up suitcase, and wearing a hot pink baseball cap with an exaggeratedly long bill.

"E.J.?" she said.

"Yes?" When she looked up at me I knew who she was.

"Glad you answered the door," she said. "Didn't wanna have to face the old bat." She moved the boy toward me with a hand on his back, and gave him the small suitcase she was carrying. "Go to your aunt E.J.," she said.

"Juney?" I asked.

"Take him," she said, and turned and walked away.

One of the most embarrassing things that can happen to a teenager happened to my husband Willis when he was fifteen years old. His mother got pregnant. This, of course, told all of his Neanderthal friends that Willis's mother, Vera, had actually had sex—and pretty damned recently to boot.

The result of this pregnancy was Willis's little brother Dusty. Willis and I met during our junior year at the University of Texas in Austin. I was young for a junior at twenty—he was old for one at twenty-three. He'd missed a few semesters here and there for bad behavior. My first trip home with him was for Dusty's promotion from Cub Scouts to Boy Scouts.

It was also the moment I fell in love with Willis; to see this oversize, long-haired, dope-smoking freek with tears of pride in his eyes for his eight-year-old brother's accomplishment totally did me in.

After our marriage, during our two-year stint in Mexico, Dusty spent his eleventh summer with us, and he was the first child-sized person I ever liked. Seeing Mexico through Dusty's eyes was a new beginning for Willis and me, and it turned into a summer of enchantment.

But Dusty wasn't like his big brother; school didn't come easily to him, and he had great difficulty learning. It took Willis years of talking to his parents before they finally admitted there was a problem and got him to a doctor to see if it could be something physical. It was; Dusty was dyslexic. But for Dusty, at fifteen, the news came too late. The hatred for learning was firmly implanted in him, and he dropped out of school at sixteen. He got a job working as a mechanic, something for which he seemed to have an aptitude.

Willis tried to get him to go to a training school or truck-driving school, but this wasn't something Dusty was interested in, and by the age of sixteen, he had begun to think of Willis as another parent, something I'm afraid Willis encouraged. So, of course, Dusty never listened to him.

By eighteen Dusty was working at the third garage of his career and drinking too much. He was running around with what Vera termed as loose women.

Then Orson Pugh, Willis's father, died. Dusty's

drinking got worse, and he stopped coming home a lot of nights until Vera threw him out.

It was a bad period, and Willis spent a lot of time driving from our home in Houston to Codderville to try to intercede with Dusty.

By his twentieth birthday, things were looking up. Graham was six years old, Megan three, and Dusty took to being an uncle like a fish to water, as old Orson would have said.

That's when seventeen-year-old Juney Trublood turned Dusty's eye. She was a true waif; a throw-away kicked out of her home by her mother and stepfather, mostly for the infraction of being more attractive to the stepfather than the mother was. Dusty fell in love and came home one evening with Juney on his arm and introduced her to Vera as his bride.

They moved into a trailer and set up house. Three weeks later they were at a bar outside of Codderville, both drinking too much. Some say Juney was flirting with Billy Campbell, others say Billy was the one who started it. Nevertheless a fight ensued; Dusty hit Billy or Billy hit Dusty. Juney got mad, and she and Dusty had words. Dusty left in a drunken huff, taking the pickup with him.

Thirty minutes later he hit a bridge abutment outside of town. He died instantly.

Vera was inconsolable, until we found out less than a month after Dusty's death that Juney was pregnant. Vera took the girl in and cared for her throughout her pregnancy.

Not to say that Vera was especially gracious about it. She didn't like Juney, and Vera is not one to be shy about speaking her mind. It was Vera's belief that if Juney had been a decent wife, she and Dusty would have been home that night, not hanging out in some bar. And if they'd been home, Dusty would still be alive. Therefore, in Vera's heart and on her lips, Juney was to blame for Dusty's death.

Garth Dustin Pugh was born one cool October evening with Vera in the delivery room. Three weeks later Juney took off for parts unknown and Vera was in hog heaven. She had her grandson all to herself.

A week after Garth's first birthday, Juney showed up unexpectedly on Vera's doorstep with a husband and a bun in the oven. And she wanted her son back.

Giving up Garth was almost as hard on Vera as losing Dusty. We'd moved back to Codderville by then, and she substituted my kids for Garth and took out her anger on me. Or so it seemed.

And now here I stood in Vera's doorway, holding the hand of a four-year-old Garth Dustin Pugh while I watched Juney walk down the street away from us, her hot pink, long-billed baseball cap the only brightness in the overcast day.

With the pins obviously out of her mouth, Vera asked from the living room, "Who is it?"

I turned and walked back in, Garth attached to me by our clasped hands.

If the pins had still been in Vera's mouth, she would have swallowed one. She pushed herself painfully up from the stool she'd been sitting on and stared at her grandson.

"Garth?" she said, her voice a whisper.

"Granma?" he asked tentatively.

I'm not sure the last time I saw Vera move that

fast. She was on that boy, as her late husband would have said, like a chicken on a June bug, picking him up and holding him to her. Tears splashed from her closed eyes as she held him.

The little boy squirmed, and I moved to them, hoping to extricate the child from his grandmother's embrace. Vera put him down and looked at him. Vera is barely five-foot-even, so she wasn't that much bigger than the four-year-old.

"Where did you come from?" she looked at me. "Where did he come from?"

I pointed at the door. "Juney just dropped him off."

"Where is she?"

"Mama had to go," Garth said. "She needs me to stay here for a while. She said you'd feed me."

"Oh, baby," Vera said. "Are you hungry?"

The little boy nodded and wiped a runny nose with the back of his hand.

"E.J., do something!" Vera said, glaring at me.

Well, this was her house, I thought. But I dutifully went into the kitchen to see what was available. In the living room I could hear Vera introducing Brenna to Garth.

I found some bologna and white bread, some mayo and potato chips, a pickle spear and an orange. I poured milk into a plastic cup kept around for my kids, and set the feast up at the kitchen table. The three trailed in from the living room.

Vera sat Garth on an old phone book on top of one of the chairs and pushed him up to the table. "Here you go, baby. Now you eat. Watch him," she said to Brenna, then grabbed my arm and dragged me into the living room.

"What is that she-devil up to now?" she demanded, no doubt referring to Juney.

"She just said take him and walked off, Vera. That's all I can tell you."

"She have a car?"

"Not that I could see. She just left, walking down the street."

"Well, she's not getting him back this time, I can guarantee you that!" Vera said. "I'll sic Jim Bob on her!"

Jim Bob was Vera's boyfriend, one of the five leading attorneys in the state of Texas—a courtly gentleman of undetermined years with a bow tie and a killer instinct. I'd sooner face a Kmart shopper frenzy than Jim Bob Honeywell in a courtroom.

"Vera, don't start—" I started, but of course wasn't able to finish.

"Don't you 'Vera' me, little miss! She's done dropped this baby in my lap one time too many! He's mine now if it harelips Texas!"

Then she turned and marched back into the kitchen, no doubt to stare at her grandson. I picked up the hall phone and called Willis. I thought he might like to know his prodigal nephew had returned.

I seemed to be the only one in thirty miles who gave a damn about Juney Trublood Pugh—whatever her other last name might be. My kids were ecstatic, Willis was overjoyed to have something of his little brother back in his life, Brenna was busy playing little mother, and Vera was—well, Vera.

I alone seemed to care about the whys of the situation. Like: Why did Juney suddenly turn up? Why did she just drop Garth off without a word? Oh, and some wheres as well: Like where in the hell was she? I called the three motels and the one bed-and-breakfast in the area and found no listing under any of the names I knew or under "Juney" at all; also no one fitting her description had checked in anyplace. Juney had dropped off Garth and walked away into oblivion.

Willis caught me as I was hanging up from what turned out to be my last call of the evening. "Don't," he said, taking my hand off the receiver. "Let Mama enjoy herself for a few days."

"But Willis—"

"Let it alone, E.J. For once in your life, just leave it alone."

Well, that's easier said than done.

Two

A little over a year ago Willis and I came into some money. Eighty-five thousand dollars to be exact. That's a lot of money to a family that basically lives from paycheck to paycheck—especially when those paychecks are sporadic, to say the least. Willis is an engineer with his own consulting firm; he gets paid when the job is done. When there's a job. I'm a romance writer; I get paid at the beginning of a book and at the end of a book. And sometimes a royalty check in between. We are not rich.

We usually have around a thousand dollars in our savings account, owing mainly to the fact that we have three children and no health insurance, and it's pretty hard to save money under those circumstances.

The $85,000 was an inheritance from our daughter Bessie's birth grandmother. Knowing Bessie's birth family had left her a considerable amount of money when they were killed, Mrs. Karnes left her relatively small insurance policy and savings to Willis and me. We'd put a big chunk of it in three money market accounts for college for Graham, Megan, and Brenna. Bessie's own money market account is overflowing.

After buying a few necessities—like a new washing machine, an upgrade for my computer, some new Reeboks, and a year's worth of health insurance—we still had about $50,000 in our savings account. And it was figuratively burning a hole in Willis's pocket.

So that's why he came home the second week Garth was at Vera's, and declared, "We need to use the money to build on to the house."

"Do what?" I demanded. I was standing at the kitchen counter, dreaming a little dream about a live-in nanny/cleaning lady who we would have to store in the garage, and wondered if my husband was again reading my mind.

"Garth is bunking on a rollaway bed in Mama's room, and Brenna keeps demanding that she sleep on the couch and Garth have her room. It's just not working. So," he said, a grin spreading across his face, "this is what we do. Come on."

He grabbed my arm and we headed out the sliding glass door into the backyard. Our house is a very traditional, square two-story. We have essentially three rooms on the first floor—living room, dining room, and kitchen/breakfast room/office (which is a closet)/utility room/half bath—and three rooms upstairs—three bedrooms and two baths, but in real estate you don't count baths. The only actual land we had was our minimal-square-foot, subdivision backyard.

"Okay, here's my plan," Willis said, pointing at the small window of the utility room. "We knock out the utility room and the kitchen window. Don't worry—there will still be plenty of light from the breakfast room. Okay, then we use the utility room as a hall into a new bedroom"—he walked backwards, dragging me with him—"that would extend to about here"—we were somewhere in the middle of the backyard—"with a big bath at the front that could connect up with the plumbing in the utility room—"

"And where do I wash clothes?" I asked, always one to dash cold water whenever possible.

"We'll just wall off a space with doors—make it a closet for the washer and dryer."

"Why?"

"This will be our room!" he said, grinning brightly. "No more running up and down stairs!"

For you, I thought. The kids would still be upstairs. *I'd* still be running up and down them.

"Then we put Brenna in our old room and Garth can have his own room at Mama's!"

I had to admit that, as a plan, it had some merit. There was only one problem. "Then what do we do when Juney comes back to get Garth?"

My husband scowled at me. "That's not going to happen," he said.

"Why not?" I asked, my figurative ice water close at hand.

"No judge in his right mind—"

"Your mother refused to fight for custody last time—"

"That was last time! We can't let Juney just keep doing this, E.J.! It's not fair to Garth, and it's not fair to Mama!"

I touched his arm. He pulled away, but I persisted. "Honey, I know that. I just think we're in a rather tentative position here. And if it does come down to a custody battle, we might need the money for that."

"Jim Bob won't charge Mama—"

"There are more expenses in something like that than just the attorney's fees."

Willis stalked back into the house like a little boy who'd just been told there was no Santa Claus. I followed him into the living room. He had the remote control in his hand, so I stood between his pointed fist and the television set.

"So why don't we just talk to some contractors and see how much?" I suggested.

"Never mind!" he said, pointing the clicker around my ample rear and bringing the TV to life.

I reached behind me and clicked the TV off at the cable box. With the contortions necessary to get the remote to turn it back on, I figured I had him for at least fifteen minutes.

"Willis, I don't think it's a *bad* idea. It's just that I think it's a little premature."

"I said never mind. It was a dumb idea."

I sat down next to him and took the remote from his hand. "You're acting like a child."

"And what is it you do every twenty-eight days?"

"You had to bring up PMS, didn't you? You just had to bring that up!"

He grabbed for the remote, and we did a little tug-of-war with the plastic clicker. He, being bigger, won. He started pushing buttons, but the TV remained blessedly silent.

"I can't believe you turned it off at the cable box," he said under his breath. "Talk about childish!"

"Are you really mad at me, or are you mad at the situation? Or are you really mad at Juney?" I asked.

"Don't you start that psychobabble with me!" he said. "Damn, sometimes I wish we'd never laid eyes on Anne Comstock!" Anne was our family therapist, who'd been helping us in more ways than I'd care to mention. Willis sighed. "I'm really, really mad at Juney. I'm mad about the situation. And I'm not all that crazy about you."

I kissed him on the nose. "Yeah, but you still think I'm cute."

"Ha!" he said.

"Willis, I don't think it's a *bad* idea—"

"Maybe I could just talk it over with Bob Neysmith—"

"Who's Bob Neysmith?"

"Offices down the hall from me. General contractor."

"Sure," I said. "Just sorta lay out the general idea—"

"Yeah, get a ballpark figure—"

"Right. Just a general discussion—"

"It's not like I'm going to sign any contracts or anything—"

"Right."

That's when our life, always precarious to begin with, turned into a living hell.

* * *

Everybody was delighted. Except me. Garth would get his own room. Brenna would get her own room. My kids would get Brenna back in the house. Vera would have her grandson all to herself. Willis would get to play with tools and make plans. And I was going to have to live eight hours a day with hordes of workmen taking over my life.

That would be, of course, after all the city, county, state, and federal guidelines, forms, and general paperwork had been filled out in triplicate and filed in the numerous places requested. Somehow Willis decided I should do that.

Willis has a problem. Since all I do is take care of the house, do all the cleaning, cooking, child rearing, carpooling, dry clean taking, etc., and write my "little stories," I should have plenty of extra time to do what he can't do while he's sitting in his office waiting for someone to call and offer him a job.

Okay, maybe I'm being a little unfair. He does the dishes.

Needless to say, the permit-getting fell to me. The one person who didn't want the work done in the first place. And then, of course, Willis discovered that the general contractor's fee for doing nothing more than hiring all the subcontractors and making sure they all showed up and did their work was going to be $10,000.

"We can do that ourselves!" he said.

We, I thought. *Yeah, right.* I said nothing.

"Really, honey. Think about it! Ten grand for what? Getting the guys to show up? You do that all the time with the washer repairman and everything else you have done around here, right?"

I said nothing.

"So we've got to be able to do as good a job and save ourselves $10,000! What you think?"

I got up and left the room.

As it was getting closer to prom night, I spent a lot of time at Vera's, helping her with Brenna's dress. It was really coming along. It was rather retro—looking just like something Audrey Hepburn might have worn in one of her fifties movies. Maybe *Funny Face.* Brenna had that beautiful-waif look about her like the late Ms. Hepburn. When Brenna got home from school, we'd practice putting her hair up in a French twist—just like Audrey.

My girls loved helping—handing me bobby pins, hair spray, oohing and ahing at Brenna's reflection in the mirror.

We were all having a great time, and it was one of the few times I didn't think about my new responsibilities as general contractor to the Pugh household.

One of the nice things about permit-gathering is that it takes so damned long for each one that I was hoping Willis would forget about the whole fiasco. But no such luck.

When the kids and I got home that night from playing with Brenna's hair, Willis met me at the door with a list.

"Okay, here's a list of plumbers. And these are the paint contractors. This is the list of electricians. Now, you need to get at least three out of each of these to show up to give bids—"

"Don't we need carpenters first?"

"I'm taking care of that," he said magnanimously.

"But how can they bid when we don't have anything to show them?"

Willis grinned and brought his right arm out from behind his back. "Viola," he said, flourishing what appeared to be blueprints. "I did this at work. It's amazing how well I remembered the stuff from the architectural classes I took back in college."

He put the blueprints down on the coffee table in the living room, sweeping all the junk off it with a swipe of his arm. I stared at the blueprint. It was of a large rectangular room with windows on two sides and what I read to be French doors leading onto the patio. Spacious-looking closets on one side and the bath on the other made a hallway leading into the room from the former utility room. He moved that blueprint to show me the bathroom blueprint. A sunken tub, a separate shower stall, two johnnie rooms, and double sinks. It looked great.

Which really pissed me off.

I wanted something to complain about. Some way I could send him back to the old drawing board. Because if I didn't, this thing was actually going to happen, and I would really have to plan my day around plumbers, electricians, carpenters, carpet layers, and sundry. And in central Texas, that meant brushing up on my almost nonexistent Spanish. And then worrying about whether I could live with a better bid because I knew this guy used illegal aliens as opposed to the more expensive guy who didn't.

Thinking quickly, I said, "Window seats?"

"Huh?" my husband said.

"I always wanted window seats in a bedroom. Could we have window seats?"

"Well, sure," he said, taking a mechanical pencil out of his pocket and quickly sketching said window seats by the placed windows.

"And built-in bookcases," I said.

"In the bedroom?"

I sighed. "Well, if you don't think so—"

The mechanical pencil went to work. "Honey, if you want built-in bookcases, we'll damn well have built-in bookcases."

"And a wall of shelves in the closets, oh, and you didn't put a linen closet in the bathroom. We'll definitely need that. And a skylight! I want a skylight in the bathroom!"

Willis gave me a suspicious glance. "The bathroom will be half under the second floor—"

"Then put the skylight under the other half," I suggested with a sweet smile.

He looked down at the blueprints, frowned, and touched the point of the mechanical pencil to his tongue. "If I move the joist and rafters three feet, use the underbeams here instead of here—"

I grinned and went into the kitchen to start supper, happy in the knowledge that nothing would happen for at least another week.

The week of bliss went by in a blink. Willis fixed the blueprints. That's when I had my inspiration.

"If we're going to do all this, why not a great room?" I said, making my eyes big in my innocence.

"A great room?" my husband said.

"Sure," I said, grabbing his mechanical pencil and bending over the blueprints. "See, we move the wall straight out here, so it goes all across the back of the house, not just half of it. Then we divide it and take out the wall of the breakfast room and then we have a den/great room that hooks on to the kitchen and breakfast room!''

I beamed at my husband.

He bent over the plans. ''Well, we can't take out that wall,'' he said, pointing at the wall of the breakfast room where the sliding glass doors went into the backyard.

''Oh,'' I said, trying to encourage a tear.

''But . . .'' he said, his gaze moving rapidly from the blueprints to the wall in question, ''. . . we could leave half walls with columns to support the beams. That would open it up, especially with the sliding glass doors gone—''

''And then move the French doors in the master bedroom to this other wall—'' I said.

''Right. Right.'' Willis bent over the plans, and I went to the kitchen to peel potatoes. Happy in my work.

Two weeks later the plans were finished, and I couldn't think of any more changes that wouldn't arouse Willis's suspicions. I mean, I *liked* the idea of an in-ground swimming pool in the master bedroom, but doubted he would go for it.

I was on the hunt for permits. It's amazing how many are necessary when building on your own property. Well, ours and the banks. That was the permit I was after on the day I drove to La Grange, thirty miles southeast, where the district office of our mortgage company was located. Even though we weren't borrowing money from the mortgage company to build the addition, it seems they had some rule or regulation about what they referred to as "substantial changes to an existing property mortgagee."

These were the last permits (last known permits) I needed to get, and since their fax machine was down, and Willis needed them *yesterday,* I was sacrificed to drive the thirty miles to La Grange, pick up the necessary paperwork, fill it out then and there, and file it wherever necessary. I had a suggestion on where Willis could file those papers, but he hung up the phone before I had a chance to explain it to him.

It was noon. The kids would be in school until three-thirty. I had no excuse not to go, according to my husband. He didn't buy the three overdue chapters, the four loads of wash, or the cat vomit in the utility room.

Mumbling obscenities under my breath, I got in the minivan and headed for La Grange.

It had been three weeks since Juney had dropped Garth off at Vera's and disappeared. Somehow it seemed more like three months. Garth had become a member of the family again so quickly he seemed never to have been gone.

My girls adored him and mothered him beyond belief; Graham had the first boy in his life to whom he could become a role model, and his behavior actually got better because of it. And Brenna, sweet Brenna, like Vera, thought the sun rose and set in the little boy's eyes.

Okay, okay. I liked him, too. He was a sweet kid. Well behaved, funny. I was doing fine keeping my distance until he crawled in my lap one day at Vera's house and snuggled up against me. "I have a tummy ache,'' he said, reaching one hand up to touch my hair and resting the other on my cheek.

That did me in. I rocked him until he fell asleep, then laid him gently in bed.

And yes, I, too, had fallen in love.

And I basically forgot about Juney. Until I drove to La Grange.

I was in the city proper, only blocks from the mortgage company office, when I passed a street corner where a woman stood holding a big cardboard sign with crude lettering that read, ''Will work for food.''

The woman, small and scrawny, wore a long-billed, hot pink baseball cap. I made an illegal U-turn one block up and parked in a parking lot on the corner where she was standing.

''Juney?'' I called, walking up to her.

She turned, surprise on her face. ''E.J.''

''Are you all right?'' I asked.

She put the sign down abruptly and tried to shield it with her body.

''I'm fine,'' she said. ''How are you?''

''Juney, don't. I saw the sign. What are you doing?''

She squatted down and began picking up her stuff—a backpack, her sign, a small cooler—and started walking away from me.

She had changed in the brief three weeks since I had last seen her. External things like dirt darkening the baseball cap, clothes obviously in need of washing—by both the look and the smell—weren't the major changes. The major changes were in her eyes, now furtive, timid, a little afraid.

"Juney, don't! Wait." I caught up with her. "I'll give you a lift anywhere you need to go."

"Get away from me, E.J., okay? I don't need your help."

I grabbed her arm and made her stop. "Okay, fine. You don't need my help." I grabbed my checkbook and tore out a deposit slip. "But here's my phone number and address if you change your mind." She wouldn't take it in her hand, so I stuffed it and a twenty-dollar bill—the only cash I had on me—in the slight opening at the top of the backpack.

Juney turned and walked away.

"Don't you want to know how Garth is?" I called after her retreating back.

There was no answer except for the stiffening of her shoulders.

"I think she's homeless," I told my husband.

He nodded. "Did you actually get the forms filed?"

I just looked at him. "Willis! Did you hear me? I said I think Juney is homeless!"

The kids were in bed, and we were having one of our rare late-night dinners together; steak, baked potato, and salad. I'd even bought some Godiva chocolates I was going to let him eat out of my navel later, but I was beginning to rethink that scenario.

"What do you want me to do about it?" he asked, not particularly graciously.

"My God, Willis! She's family!"

"Not mine," he said, doggedly returning to his food.

I pulled his plate out from under his fork. "How

can you say that? She was Dusty's wife! She's Garth's mother!''

Willis put his fork down and stared at me, his fists clenched atop the table. ''She was married to my brother for three weeks, E.J. Three weeks! And because of her he's dead—''

''Willis—''

''Stop! Because of her Dusty is dead. And as far as her being Garth's mother, I'd say she's a damned poor one. She ran off and left him for his first year of life, and now she's done the same thing again. That woman is not my family, and if she's homeless, I'd say she probably brought it on herself and I really don't care.''

''You realize she was practically the same age as Brenna when she and Dusty got married?'' I asked.

Willis didn't answer; he just reached for his plate and went back to stuffing his face.

''Only seventeen years old, Willis. Just a baby herself. Remember the stupid things you did when you were seventeen? Hell, remember the stupid things you did when you were twenty-six?''

''I never abandoned my children. Remember when she came and got Garth when he was a year old? She was pregnant then, right? Where's that baby? Who did she abandon that baby with, E.J.? And, in case you didn't notice, she's not seventeen anymore. She's a twenty-two-year-old mother of two. When do you want her to start taking responsibility for her own actions?''

I jumped up from the table and starting clearing dishes. ''I swear,'' I said, ''I think you're turning into a Republican!''

"Do Republicans have the market cornered on common sense and decency?" he asked, rising from the table, hands on hips, voice raised.

"I'm not going to argue with you about this!" I said.

"Excuse me? I think that's exactly what we're doing!" he yelled.

"My God, Willis, she's homeless!"

"And just how do you know that? Because she was holding one of those damned 'will work for food' signs? That doesn't prove shit! For all you know it could be a con! Or she could be part of one of those weird cults!"

"I'm going to find Juney and I'm going to help her and you can go to hell!"

He glared at me. "You'd help her to the detriment of your own family?"

"What does that mean? That if I help her she can get her kid back from your mother? Damn it, Willis, it's *her* kid!"

"Stay out of it, E.J.," Willis said, his voice icy cold. "I won't let you or anyone else hurt my mother anymore."

He turned and walked out of the kitchen. Seconds later I heard his heavy tread on the stairs. I leaned back against the counter and took a deep breath.

This is some serious shit, I told myself. My choices were simple: lend a helping hand to a homeless woman and destroy my family, or walk away.

It was going to be a long night.

Three

I'm ashamed to admit that I did nothing. I tried to fool myself by saying I had no idea where to look for her, but even I didn't fall for that. I tried to console myself that it probably was a scam, like Willis had said, and that she was living in the lap of luxury and just begging on the streets for kicks. I didn't buy that one either.

I kept remembering her eyes, her guarded, frightened eyes.

I finally had to admit to myself that I didn't want to rock the boat. It had taken many long, hard years to get to the place where Vera and I were now—truly friends. Taking sides at this point—and there was no doubt in my mind that helping Juney would be construed as taking sides by my mother-in-law—would jeopardize all that and maybe more.

Willis had never said much about Juney—when she married Dusty, or when she moved in with Vera during her pregnancy. He'd never bad-mouthed her after she ran away and left Garth with his grandmother. And he'd been fairly quiet when she took Garth back when he was a year old.

But his silence on the subject had obviously been deceptive. He definitely had feelings about Juney Trublood—none of them good.

I tried not to think about her as prom approached. I had entirely too much to do, and thinking about Juney was not on my priority list.

It was the Friday before the prom on Saturday, and I had to go into Codderville and pick up Brenna's shoes, which were being dyed to match her dress, go to the market, and get the ingredients for guacamole for seventy-five for the all-night after-prom party Brenna and her boyfriend Trent were going to, and call Trent and make sure the corsage he was getting was going to match the midnight blue taffeta dress—that still needed hemming and a zipper. Not that I was going to hem or zip—that was Vera's department, but I did need to make sure she got it done. I saw myself largely in a supervisory position.

When the phone rang as I was heading toward the door, I almost didn't answer it. How many times has that happened? Where you've almost escaped, then stopped to answer the phone, only to have it truly mess up your day—or even ruin your life.

"Hello?" I said, car keys in hand, purse on my shoulder.

"Pugh, it's Luna," she said. Elena Luna is my

next-door neighbor, probably my closest friend—though we both try not to admit that—and a detective in the Codderville Police Department.

"Luna, I was just walking out the door—"

"I need you to stop by the station. It's important."

My mind flew ninety miles an hour. Unpaid parking tickets? A moving violation? What had I done now? I'd already had the dubious pleasure of seeing the inside of the Codderville jail and didn't have time for any repeat performances.

"What's up?" I asked.

"I need you to stop by the station. I'll tell you then."

"Luna, I haven't got time—" I started, but she'd hung up.

I slammed the phone down and headed out the door. The shoe store where Brenna's shoes were being dyed wasn't that far from the courthouse. I could swing by, get the shoes, run in and see what Luna wanted.

Late May in much of the country is still considered spring; in central Texas, although the calendar may call it spring, it is definitely summer. The bluebonnets, the Texas state flower, that grace the sides of the highway from mid-March through April to early May, depending upon the rain, were long gone, replaced by later blooming wildflowers.

Because of the forward thinking of former first lady Ladybird Johnson, the Texas Highway Department has a program whereby they sprinkle mixed wildflower seeds on the roadways and medians every time they mow or pick up trash. Not only does this beautify the roads of the state, it saves money. With wildflowers growing well into July—before the intense heat burns them up—the parks department doesn't need to spend time and money mowing.

As it was still fairly early in the day—only around 10 A.M.—I rolled down the windows in the minivan and let nature have its way with my mess of carrot red hair—as if it hadn't already had its way with it from birth—and could smell the flowers on the sides of the road and listen to the birdsong as I drove into Codderville, pretending there was no reason to be nervous about my summons to the police station.

I picked up Brenna's shoes, paid entirely too much for the privilege of having them dyed midnight blue, and drove the three blocks to the station. I parked and stared at the building.

What had I done? I asked myself. Then I remembered. A speeding ticket I forgot to pay two months ago! *But that was in the county and issued by the sheriff's department, not the Codderville Police Department,* I told myself. *Yeah,* my other self said, *but maybe Luna's pimping for Lance Moncrief, the new sheriff. You know she thinks he's hot.*

I sat there longer than necessary before finally talking myself into getting out of the van. Luna saw me as I opened the side door into the police station.

She grabbed my arm. "Come on," she said, taking me back out the door.

"I didn't do it," I said.

"Shut up, Pugh."

She dragged me to her unmarked squad car, where her sometimes partner, Buster Murphy, sat behind the wheel, a Butterfinger stuck in his mouth like a cigar.

Luna opened the back door, and said, "Get in."

I just looked at her.

"Get in," she said, a tad irritably.

"Look, I meant to pay the ticket," I said. "I just forgot. Honest!"

Buster laughed. Not a good sign I thought.

Luna shook her head. "Get in the car," she repeated.

I got in the backseat of the squad car. Which is not exactly a nice place to be. You can't roll the windows down, and there are no door handles with which to attempt escape.

Buster put the car in gear and headed out of the parking lot. All was silent in the interior of the car as we sped out of town. About two miles outside the city limits of Codderville, which is definitely country, we turned on a farm-to-market road, drove for about a mile, turned onto a smaller road going toward the river, then abruptly turned onto a rutted dirt road—nothing more than two car tracks with weeds and wildflowers growing in the middle. This road stopped at a clearing near the water, where three sheriff's cars stood empty.

Great, I thought. *I was right. It's about the ticket. Maybe they've stopped fining people and now they're just throwing speeders directly into the Colorado.*

After Buster stopped the car, I waited like a lady for someone to come open my door, which Luna, ever the gentleman, did. She helped me out, then, with Luna and Buster flanking me front and rear, we walked into the woods, following a small footpath into the dense foliage.

Central Texas is not the desolate wasteland a lot of people—mostly Yankees—think about when they hear Texas. We have desolate wasteland, but that's mostly in the panhandle and in extreme west Texas. The area we walked into was dense with huge, towering oak trees, wild mimosa, large native pecan trees just turning green, and even a pine or two, thanks to birds with bowel problems. The underbrush was thick as we made our way single file down the dirt track.

We finally came to a clearing. Sheriff's personnel were scattered here and there, as were piles of garbage. At least at first glance they appeared to be piles of garbage. Further study proved them to be people's belongings—bedrolls, sacks of clothing, some foodstuffs. In a corner of the clearing, stuck between two large pecan trees, was a small structure, a lean-to, made of corrugated iron, street signs, and cardboard.

Most of the sheriff's department activity seemed to be centered around the lean-to. In the melee of tan uniforms, one stood out. I would recognize Lance Moncrief's backside blindfolded in a tub of Jell-O. Actually, I'd love to be near Lance Moncrief's backside blindfolded and in a tub of Jell-O. But that's another story entirely. On hearing us walk up, he turned. John Wayne should have looked so good in a uniform.

I smiled and wiggled my fingers at the sheriff.

He doffed his cap. "Miz Pugh. Always a pleasure." Which I knew he didn't mean. Our last encounter hadn't been pleasurable for *him.* "You recognize this lady?" he asked, stepping away from the lean-to and giving me my first glimpse of what all the commotion was about.

A woman—small, scrawny, wearing lots of baggy clothing—lay on the ground, the back of her head a bloody mess. Next to her head was a long-billed, hot pink baseball cap.

"We found this clutched in her hand," the sheriff said, handing me a crumpled piece of paper. It was a deposit slip for my bank account. More than likely the one I had given Juney more than a week before. "You recognize it?"

"Of course," I said, anger tinging my words. I can't help it. Death makes me angry. Juney's death made me furious. "It's a deposit slip from my checkbook."

"Why do you think this woman had it?" he asked.

"Because I gave it to her!" I said. "She's my sister-in-law!"

Footsteps sounded behind us, and we all turned to see the county coroner come into the clearing. This month's county coroner (the job seems to be up for grabs most of the time) was a fastidious little woman named Ruthanne Turner who ran the flower shop over on First Street and thought running for coroner would get more people to come into her shop. She'd been wrong.

We don't have a medical examiner. Most small counties in Texas don't. When a murder or death by misadventure turns up, the body is usually shipped to the nearest county with a morgue and medical examiner. In our case Austin and Dr. Bayardo.

In the meantime, Ruthanne Turner slipped on latex gloves and knelt next to the body, a grimace on her face. "Is she dead?" she asked the assembled crowd.

"That's for you to determine, Ruthanne," Lance Moncrief said.

Ruthanne felt for a pulse. "Well, I'd say yeah, I think she's dead."

"I agree with you," the sheriff said. "About five hours give or take, don't you think, Ruthanne?"

She stood up and hastily removed her gloves. "That sounds about right to me, Sheriff," she said.

I could feel my anger building. Nobody cared. Ruthanne obviously found the whole thing distasteful; and the sheriff, great buns or no, was thinking only of how expeditiously he could wrap the whole thing up. Juney lay dead in front of all these people, and nobody cared. Would a four-year-old boy be the only person alive to grieve for her?

Moncrief made a motion with his hand, and one of the deputies rolled the body over, faceup.

I stared. I moved closer.

It wasn't Juney.

I stood leaning against Luna's squad car, fanning myself with my hand. I'd just vomited in the bushes, and I wasn't feeling great.

Sheriff Lance Moncrief, Luna, and her partner Buster Murphy were all standing in front of me staring at me.

"I tell you it's not her," I repeated for the ump teenth time.

"But you said it was."

"Yes. But I was wrong. When I saw the face I realized it wasn't her."

"What made you think it was?" Luna asked.

"The deposit slip, of course," I said, trying to breathe through my mouth and not my nose. The wind was coming from the direction of the dead body, and I was beginning to think the sheriff had been wrong with his five-hour estimate.

Luna folded her arms and looked at me. "There's more," she said. "You recognized something the minute you saw the body—before Lance showed you the deposit slip."

Take it from me, never make friends with a cop—especially if you're in the habit of having friends and family get in trouble from time to time.

"Uh-uh," I said.

She just looked at me. There's a certain look Luna has mastered—not unlike that certain look of my mother's—the one that tells you you better fess up now before the shit really hits the fan.

"The baseball cap," I said resignedly. "I saw my sister-in-law wearing one like it twice."

"What's your sister-in-law's name?" Moncrief asked.

Well, he had me there. "Juney. I don't know her last name."

The officers all exchanged glances—as if I'd fib. "Really," I said. "Her maiden name was Trublood. She married Willis's little brother, then her last name was Pugh, then he died and she married someone else and I have no idea what his name was. And I don't know which of the three names she might be going under now."

"Did you recognize the victim?" Moncrief asked.

I shook my head. "I've never seen her before."

"But she looked like your sister-in-law? This Juney?"

"Same size. I couldn't tell the hair color, but Juney's hair color changes more often than her last name. I guess it was just the baseball cap and then the deposit slip that made me think it was her.''

''Where does your sister-in-law live?'' Moncrief asked.

I looked around. For all I knew, this was where she lived. ''I don't know,'' I said.

Finally, I sighed, and told them everything I knew, from the minute she dropped Garth off at Vera's until the time I saw her on the street corner in LaGrange with the ''will work for food'' sign.

I stopped talking as the paramedics brought the body out on a stretcher, in a body bag.

''Come on back to the scene, Miz Pugh. See if you see anything might have belonged to this Juney girl,'' Moncrief said.

Deputies had been moving the litter of personal effects into a pile. There was a duffel bag filled with women's torn and stained underwear, a shopping bag full of rotting bananas, sacks of clothes, torn and smelly blankets, a pillow with a hole in the corner and most of the feathers missing, a Dopp kit containing a sliver of soap and a tiny empty bottle of shampoo, and, for some unknown reason, a birdcage full of balled up newspaper.

The debris of human life. All that was left of someone's ''stuff,'' the stuff that gives us our identity.

A cold shiver ran down my spine. Like so many Americans, my family and I have often lived just two paychecks away from the very clearing I was standing in. Seeing the debris left behind by the person or persons living here, I wondered where the other stuff was.

Maybe I'm too connected to my possessions, I thought, but I couldn't stand the thought of not having my children's baby albums, my grandmother's afghan, my books, my albums and CDs—hell, even my Tupperware. How would I survive without my nightly ritual of a leisurely bath, lotion on my hands and feet, then lying down on my extrathick down pillow between cool, soft cotton sheets?

The big things, like how to get the children to school, keep the family together, clean and feed ourselves—those loomed too large to contemplate. I was stuck on the stuff. Where did all the stuff go? How do you pare down your life to a sliver of soap and a bag of rotting bananas?

I looked inside the crooked little house, leaning between the pecan trees. More rotted bedding, a heap of filthy clothes. Then I saw a backpack. I knelt next to it and unzipped the top. Inside were more clothes, cleaner and better cared for than what I'd seen so far, toiletries, and a framed picture. A picture of my nephew Garth.

I stood and held the backpack out to the sheriff. "This is Juney's," I said. "There's a picture of my nephew in here."

He took the pack and started pawing through her stuff, making me feel guilty for having given it to him. If that was all Juney had left, he had no right to be touching it, to be putting his hands on her panties and bras, touching her soap and shampoo, handling Garth's picture.

It hadn't completely escaped me that the sheriff was thinking of Juney as his prime suspect in the murder of the woman whose body had just been found. I'd been known to jump on the bandwagon in protecting people against such charges, but could I do that with Juney? Did I know her well enough to say she couldn't have done this? Did I know her at all?

The answer was no. The unhappy girl who lived in Vera's house for seven months, awaiting the birth of her baby, wasn't the same person as the woman who left Garth at Vera's and walked off into the limbo of homelessness.

And even if she was, I hadn't known the girl well either. I'd brought her the baby clothes Graham had long since outgrown, had talked to her about the pregnancy and what to expect with childbirth, had listened to her complain (and silently agreed) about Vera. But we hadn't been close. I hadn't really known her.

And I certainly didn't know her now—almost five years later. I heard Willis's voice in my ear: ''What kind of woman walks off and leaves her child?''

But women did that all the time—decent, hard-working, loving women who, due to circumstances of health or finance, found themselves leaving their children with someone else—hopefully for just a little while.

That's what I had thought was going on with Juney. Down on her luck, she'd dropped Garth off with Vera, just until she could get back on her feet. That's what I'd been telling myself, over and over and over again. Now there was a dead body in the woods, Juney's backpack, baseball cap, and my deposit slip, all found on that dead body.

It didn't take a rocket scientist to connect the two.

Four

"You been messin' with that trash?'' Vera spit at me.

The trash she was referring to, of course, was Juney, mother of Vera's beloved grandson.

''I haven't been messing with anything or anyone, Vera. I just saw her when I went to La Grange—''

''Well, she can stay there! I'd rather she were farther away, but La Grange is far enough if she just stays there!''

''Vera, I think she's in trouble—''

''Good,'' my mother-in-law said, jumping up from the kitchen table where we'd been drinking coffee and going to the refrigerator. She began taking stuff off the shelves and placing them on the counter. All the stuff. She was going to clean the refrigerator in the middle of our conversation.

"You don't mean that—" I started.

"The hell I don't!" she said, tossing a plastic bowl of leftovers in the sink. I'd known Vera for seventeen years. That's the second time, I believe, that I've heard her use a cussword.

"Vera, she's homeless—"

"Ha! I'm not surprised! Just like her to end up on the streets with the winos and crazies! 'Cause that's what she is! Crazy!"

Luckily it was Saturday afternoon, and Brenna had taken all the kids to the movies. She needed to kill some time before starting to get ready for the prom and had offered this. So Vera and I were alone in the house, and she was not pulling any punches.

"Vera, a woman was killed—"

"Who?"

"I don't know—"

"Then what has that got to do with the price of beans?" she asked, glaring at me.

"Juney may have been involved."

Vera shut the refrigerator door and sat back down at the table. "Tell me," she said.

I told her everything about my excursion into the woods with the Codderville police and Lance "Great Butt" Moncrief.

She started making "tsk, tsk" sounds when I described the debris in the clearing. "No excuse for that," she said. "Cleanliness is next to godliness, and it don't take squat to wash a few clothes."

Cleanliness may be next to godliness, I thought, *but it's also next to impossible when you're living on the streets.* But I didn't say it. It's amazing how much I *don't* say around Vera. Me, with a mouth as big as all outdoors.

"So Juney killed some other crazy woman out in the woods." She sighed and stood up, heading back for the refrigerator. "Can't say I'm surprised. Girl never was stable. I told you that before, and I'm telling you that now! So you, Miss Gotta Stick My Nose in Everybody's Business, you just stay clear of her, you hear me?"

"Vera—"

"Don't 'Vera' me, girl. Stay out of it!"

"I can't promise that," I said softly.

"You mess with trash, you become trash." Vera slammed the refrigerator door and marched out of the kitchen, slamming every door between there and her bedroom.

I remembered I'd left Brenna's newly dyed shoes at my house. I went to Vera's bedroom door and knocked. There was no response. "I need to run home a minute and pick up Brenna's shoes," I said. "I'll be right back." Still no response. "Vera, did you hear me?"

"I heard you," she said.

"Okay, I'll see you in a minute then." No response.

I stared at the door for a second, then turned and left.

Why can't life just be easy? I thought as I drove over the Colorado to my subdivision of Black Cat Ridge. *Why all the complications? Wasn't it tough enough dealing with a husband, three kids, three cats, a dog, and a mother-in-law? Not to mention a mortgage, a writing career, the PTA, carpooling, and grocery shopping with coupons? Why did I have to keep getting involved with shit like this?* I asked myself.

And then I answered myself. I didn't have to. Nobody was asking me to. Actually, everybody was asking me not to. Willis wanted me out of it, Vera wanted me out of it, and even Juney didn't want my help. So why was I so determined to get involved?

I let out a big sigh. I didn't have to get involved. I could get Brenna's shoes, take them to Vera's, help Brenna with her hair and dress for the prom, and stand by ready to take pictures when Trent showed up with the corsage. I had my kids and my husband and my life. Nobody else needed me.

Sure, there were homeless out there, but what kind of ego did it take to think I could solve the problem single-handedly? I couldn't. I resolved then and there to do the grown-up, Republican thing. I'd go home and write a check.

There are all sorts of clichés that fit what happened next: "The best laid plans of mice and men . . . ," "The road to hell is paved with good intentions," and my personal favorite, "No good deed goes unpunished."

When I arrived at my house, my neighbor Elena Luna was walking away from my front door. I pulled into the driveway, and she stood waiting as I got out of the car.

"Where you been?" she asked.

"I wasn't aware I needed to check in with you," I said.

She grinned. "Anybody running around with unpaid moving violations should be watched over."

"That was a joke," I said, moving quickly to the front door.

"Funny, but the sheriff's department's computer is in on the joke. You better pay that ticket, Pugh," she said, following me into the house.

"The check's in the mail. Cold or hot?"

"Hot tea sounds good," she said.

She settled at the breakfast-room table while I put the water on, got the teapot, and put some Earl Grey in the tea ball. I grabbed mugs, Equal for me, sugar for her, and the cream. When the water boiled, I poured it into the pot and brought everything to the table, letting the tea steep.

"So what's going on with the home remodeling?" Luna asked.

I rolled my eyes and shook my head. "Don't ask," I said. "I'm afraid we're really going through with it."

"Tell Willis if they hurt my yard or fence, I'll sue his pants off."

I laughed. "That won't impress him. He thinks you've been trying to get into his pants for years."

It was Luna's turn to roll her eyes. "A little harmless flirtation, and men immediately think the worst."

"Or as they would say, the best." I knew we were both beating around a bush—I just wasn't sure which bush. "So," I said, "what's up?"

"We've identified the body we found in the woods," she said.

This is none of your business, I told myself. *Tell Luna you don't want to know. Get up now. Flee!* "Who was she?" I asked instead.

"Patricia Glancy, better known as Trish."

"Glancy . . . Glancy. . . .That name's familiar," I said.

"Like in Glancy Industries out on Brenham Highway," Luna said.

"Oh! That Glancy. What the hell was she doing living in the woods?"

"We found out who she was because one of the guys at our office arrested her a couple of times. Drunk and disorderly. Disturbing the peace. Except Trish wasn't a drinker." Luna touched her index finger to her temple. "Schizophrenic."

"Why wasn't she hospitalized?" I asked.

"She was. A lot. Her folks would put her in one of those fancy hospitals for a ninety-day involuntary, then she'd be out and on the streets."

"Her folks must be devastated," I said, pouring the tea.

"More likely relieved."

I gave her a look. "I know, I know," she said. "I'm a cold-assed bitch."

"Your words, not mine. But accurate nonetheless."

"No telling what she did to your sister-in-law to get her that riled up. But I hear Trish was a piece of work a lot of the time—"

"What has my sister-in-law got to do with it?" I demanded.

Luna gave me a look. "She's our best suspect, Pugh. You gotta know that. All her stuff's there, except she's not. No evidence that anyone else was camped out there except those two." Luna sipped her tea. "You heard anything from Juney?" she asked, her voice dripping innocence.

''No,'' I said.

''And you'd tell me if you had, right?''

''Of course,'' I said, burying my nose in my tea mug.

''By the way,'' Luna said, standing, ''the only help we need from you on this is to tell us if your sister-in-law calls you. Nothing else. No interfering this time. Got it?''

''Of course,'' I said, indignation tainting my voice.

Luna shook her head. ''I said what I had to say. It's out of my hands now.'' With those parting words, she was out the back door, headed for her house.

I sat there sipping my tea. When that was gone, I poured another cup, liberally dosing it with Equal and cream. I need calories to help my brain work. I went to the refrigerator, opening the cabinet above it where I keep my stash of chocolate. I found a half-full bag of Nestles Buncha Crunch and took it to the table, alternating sips of tea with bites of chocolate-and-rice crunchies.

Luna had said Juney was their best suspect. I found it hard to believe that Juney could do such a thing, but I'd been wrong before. There were a lot of reasons for people to kill, reasons you or I might not think deserving, but it happens. In my life, it had happened too often.

I didn't know Patricia Glancy or her family. But I knew how they were feeling. I knew the pain and the horror of losing someone you love to violence. And I knew the overpowering need to seek justice.

When Bessie's birth family was killed, I'd been consumed with that need, so consumed that I often thought what I was really looking for was revenge, not justice. The deaths of Terry and Roy Lester and Bessie's brother Aldon and sister Monique will haunt me for the rest of my life, and my sweet daughter Bessie will always be a reminder, no matter how much I love her, no matter how much she is now really and truly mine.

Because Bessie lived, Terry and Roy have a legacy, one that Willis and I are bound by law and love to protect, honor, and cherish.

What did the Glancys have of their daughter? What was left except the empty memories of pain and mental disease? Schizophrenia comes usually in late teens, early adulthood. So maybe they had her early years, years to remember her happy and disease-free. But they would want their ounce of flesh—their justice—their revenge.

And Juney was in the spotlight for receiving that. Whether she was guilty or not.

I sighed as I realized I was breaking another pledge to myself. I knew I was getting involved.

I looked in the Codderville/Black Cat Ridge residential phone directory under Glancy. They were listed at an address in Black Cat Ridge. I knew where the street was and decided I could just take a quick look on my way back to Vera's.

Black Cat Ridge is broken into villages with price tags attached. It went from the $75,000–$80,000 village called Robin Hood to the $250,000–$500,000 village called Sherwood Forest. We lived in Friar Tuck—or more succinctly, the $85,000–$125,000 village. The street the Glancys lived on, Maid Marian

Circle, was in Sherwood Forest, the high end of the neighborhood. I drove the mile and a half from my medium-priced village to the exclusive village and easily found Maid Marian Circle and the number for the Glancy house. It was a huge Tara-type place on two large lots, about an acre and a half total. A brand-new Mercedes was parked under a porte cochere that led to a garage in the back. The landscaping was lush, and I was sure was partway responsible for the yearly water shortages Black Cat Ridge was prone to.

But the very nicest thing about the Glancy house was that it was right next door to Liz Jones's house. Liz Jones and I had been on several committees together at our church. Although we didn't run in the same social circle, I liked her and thought she liked me. Maybe not enough for a casual drop-in, but I thought I'd call later. Maybe see if I could drop over on Monday. I smiled to myself, then thought, *There you go again, you're getting involved. No, I'm not,* I assured myself. *I just haven't seen Liz in a while. We have a lot to catch up on. Liar,* my other self said. I had to agree.

The kids were back from the movies, and Brenna was pacing the floor when I walked into my mother-in-law's house.

"Where have you been?" Brenna demanded, arms akimbo, face drawn in a frown.

I held up the shoes. "I left these at home," I said. "Sorry. You ready to get started?"

"Miss Vera's pissed about something and won't come out of her room! Garth ate too much junk at the movies, and he's in the bathroom vomiting! The girls are fighting over *something*—God only knows what with those two—and Graham is being a pain in the butt.''

I grinned. ''This should keep you celibate for a few years.''

Brenna blushed. ''Gawd, E.J.!''

I went into the bathroom to check on Garth, who had fallen asleep with his head on the toilet lid, vomity drool staining his chin. I cleaned him up and carried him to Vera's room and knocked on the door.

''Your grandson needs to take a nap,'' I said.

The door opened, Vera took Garth from my arms and butt-slammed the door in my face. That's the thing about Vera—she's always had such a lovely disposition.

I went into Brenna's bedroom, where I found my daughters. They were obviously over their disagreement. They were sitting in the middle of Brenna's floor, gleefully throwing little torn-off pieces of Silly Putty at each other. Colorful globs of pink, blue, and green were stuck in strawberry blond and dark brown hair respectively—and on the rug, Brenna's comforter, and the walls.

''Stop,'' I said. ''Clean it all up. Now!''

''Oh, Mom!'' wailed twin voices.

''Now!''

I shut the door and headed into the only room I hadn't yet been in—the kitchen. My son Graham was sitting at the table, his arms crossed and his bottom lip protruding.

''What's the matter with you?'' I asked.

''Brenna sucks,'' he said.

Well, I thought. *When this kid gets over a crush, he really gets over a crush.*

"Why?" I asked.

"She's a bitch," my eleven-year-old said.

"Don't call her that."

"Well, she is."

"Be that as it may," I said, "don't use the word."

Graham rolled his eyes.

"What did she do that made you so mad?" I asked.

His arms got tighter across his chest, and his lips thinned into a grimace. "Nothing," he said.

I smiled really big. "Good. Then don't be mad."

He rolled his eyes again.

"Don't get me involved, Graham, unless you actually want me involved. And if you want me involved, then you have to tell me what's wrong," I reasoned, just like our family therapist had taught me.

He got up and stormed out of the room, saying over his shoulder, "Oh, bugger off."

Well, I thought, *no more PBS for him!*

Brenna was still pacing the living room. "Why's Graham so bent out of shape?" I asked her.

She threw up her hands. "I don't know! The girls and I were talking about the prom tonight, and he just started acting like a brat!"

I rolled *my* eyes. "Brenna, come on!"

"What?" she said, looking genuinely perplexed.

I had no idea where my son was, so I suggested she and I fight the canine conspiracy in the backyard. Two of Vera's three dogs and our one dog were having a wonderful time ganging up on the third, who was peeing all over himself in an attempt to gain favor. I yelled at the bad dogs, soothed the ganged-up-on dog, and sat down with Brenna on the steps of Vera's back porch.

"Honey," I said, "I can't believe you haven't figured out yet that my son has a giant crush on you."

"Oh, that," Brenna said. "I know that, E.J. But—"

"But nothing. You're going to the prom with Trent—"

"Graham adores Trent—"

"As your friend. Not as your date for a dress-up dance and an all-night party to boot."

Brenna rolled her eyes. There was a lot of that going around. "So what am I supposed to do?"

I shrugged and patted her bare knee. "Nothing you can do, I guess. Talk to him if you think it will do any good—"

"Oh, talking to Graham is always a joy," she said, sarcasm dripping.

"Just try to think of his feelings, honey, that's all I'm asking."

Brenna sighed. "I know. I will." She hugged me. "I'm sorry."

I hugged her back. "Nothing to be sorry about. It's not your fault you're so damned cute."

Brenna pushed me away and jumped up, taking a pose. "Don't hate me because I'm beautiful."

Pointing at Brenna, I said to the dogs, "Sic her!"

All four sat down and grinned at me, tongues lolling and tails wagging.

They, like everybody else in my life, minded so well.

Five

It was the Monday of the third week before school let out. Or the third week before hell on earth, as I like to call summer vacations.

Things had gone fairly well on prom night. Brenna had been beautiful, Trent had been handsome, the girls had been overjoyed, and Graham had been pissed. Same old, same old.

Vera had come out of her room long enough to take pictures of Brenna and Trent in their finery, kiss and hug Willis as if she hadn't seem him in a week, and glare daggers at me. None of this, of course, fazed my husband. As long as he's on somebody's good side, he doesn't care whose.

Willis took Trent aside and discussed manly things like no drinking, no drugs, no speeding, no leaving the after-hours party, and no touching.

I helped Trent pin on Brenna's corsage, then we all waved (except Graham, of course) as they made their way to the shiny new Cadillac Trent's father—a car dealer—had dug up for the occasion.

Later, after I got the kids in bed and Willis comfy on the sofa in front of the TV, I took the 150 pounds of guacamole—okay, I exaggerate—to the after-prom-party location at around ten, grateful that all I'd had to do was swim in green slime for a few hours rather than actually chaperone the all-night affair—and I use that term loosely.

Sunday—because I have a mean streak about a mile wide—we all trooped back over to Vera's and woke up Brenna to find out how everything went. She was not amused.

So now it was Monday. The kids were in school. The animals were fed. And I'd made a date for a little coffee klatch with Liz Jones for 10 A.M.

Her house, right next door to the Glancys' on Maid Marian Circle, was a huge, traditional two-story with wings. I'd been in it before for committee meetings and church socials and had always felt warm and welcome. Liz's house is a lot like she is—big and open and welcoming. She'd raised five healthy, happy, well-adjusted kids in that house, and it showed. Liz was one of the few people I'd ever met who seemed truly at ease with herself and her life. After knowing Liz for ten minutes, you forgot—if you'd noticed at all—that she was a great deal overweight. What you noticed was her smile, her warmth, her humor, and her honesty.

She was adored by her children and worshiped by her husband, an OB/GYN who had delivered half of the people in the greater Codderville/Black Cat Ridge area.

Liz was one of the few people I knew who, when you told her something you were going to say was confidential, you knew she would take it to her grave. In the same way, you knew if she told you something, it had been checked out front and back and attested to in writing by at least three eyewitnesses. Liz didn't gossip—but boy, did she have some great truths to tell.

She opened the door to my ring and gave me a bear hug in greeting. "Girl, you haven't been to church in a coon's age. Where have you been?"

"Life, Liz, life," I said, following her into the spacious foyer.

"Come on into the kitchen," she said. "I've made kolaches and cinnamon coffee."

I followed her and my nose to the back of the house and the huge kitchen. It was everything a kitchen should be: large, with double ovens—plus a brick oven for baking—two sinks on opposite ends of the room, a restaurant-style refrigerator and cooktop, hanging copper-bottomed pots and pans, hanging baskets of ferns, and ropes of peppers and garlic that she actually used. A huge round table dominated the room, with chairs enough for Liz and her husband, their five kids plus spouses, and the new grandkids when they came. A large brick fireplace and two easy chairs atop a hooked rug took up one corner, and a bulletin board larger than half my kitchen took up one wall, complete with hand-painted artwork by various Jones offspring—first and second generation.

We settled down at the table with kolaches and coffee. "So," Liz said grinning, "what's up?"

"Can't I just drop by for a—"

"Visit? Uh-uh," she said. "I mean you can, anytime you want. But you don't. So something's up. Tell all."

I did. I started with Juney's knock on Vera's front door and ended with my conversation on Saturday with Luna, wherein I found out the identity of the woman in the woods.

Liz nodded her head. "I heard," she said, a grave look on her face. "Poor Trish. She and Connie"—Liz's third child—"were in the same class. They were friends in junior high, and ran in the same crowd in high school, although they weren't as close then."

"Liz, I've got to admit I don't know my sister-in-law that well, but for her little boy's sake, I have to assume she didn't do this."

Liz nodded. "That's the only thing you can think, E.J. She's family."

"What can you tell me about the Glancys?" I asked.

Liz took a bite of kolache and another sip of her coffee. Swallowing, she said, "Well, we knew Edgar and Madge before we all moved here from Codderville. Like I said, the girls were friends in junior high, and we ran in the same circles. I can't say we were best friends or anything, but I always admired Madge. She was a class act. She died of breast cancer when Connie and Trish were, what? Freshmen in high school, I think. That's when things started going wrong for Trish. She and her mom were really close.

Edgar tried, but he's an old-fashioned man. One of the type who never really had much to do with his child. But he loved Trish, and he tried everything he could think of,'' Liz said, then grimaced. ''Mostly everything he could buy. If you could spend money on it, Edgar could deal with it.'' She shook her head. ''Then he started having Mona come around to the house—''

''Mona?'' I asked.

''His office manager. At least she was then. Now she's the second Mrs. Glancy. She would come by and try to help out with Trish. Connie was still going over there some then and said that Trish just kept getting weirder and weirder. Finally, Connie refused to go over there anymore. Said she couldn't stand being around Mona, who was there all the time by then. More coffee?''

Liz got up to fill our cups, still talking. ''That's when they started building Black Cat Ridge and we needed a bigger house so we had one built up here. Then, lo and behold, six months after we moved in, the lot next door—actually two lots next door—started having a house built on it. I'd lost track of Edgar once we moved here and then I found out he and Mona had gotten married. Trish must have been, oh, sixteen by then. Well, they moved in, and Edgar kept trying to get us over there, which we did, of course, but I have to say Connie was right. That Mona's a piece of work. Never did care for her. Of course, that could be because she just wasn't Madge, you know? Madge was a wonderful woman.''

''Trish didn't get along with Mona?''

Liz shook her head. ''Not at all. I mean, these

houses aren't all that close together, and what with central air-conditioning, the windows are closed most of the time, but sometimes you could still hear them screaming at each other. But when the girls graduated things started looking up; Trish had been accepted to Stanford and was really excited about it. Then, halfway into the first semester, Edgar flew out to California and brought her back. I found out later she'd been missing for almost a week and he found her in a homeless shelter. That was the real beginning, I guess."

"What happened when she came home?" I asked.

Liz shook her head, her shoulders bent in sorrow. "It just got progressively worse. Edgar took her to psychiatrist after psychiatrist, doctor after doctor. She was diagnosed with everything from a brain tumor to schizophrenia."

"So you're not sure she was actually schizophrenic?"

She nodded. "Oh, that diagnosis finally stuck. It definitely wasn't a brain tumor. I heard her talking to herself on several occasions," Liz said. "And she always seemed to get an answer."

"Did her dad get her on medication?"

"Of course. But you obviously don't know a lot about mental illness. I have a brother who used to be manic-depressive. Now, of course, he's bipolar." She laughed. "I wish they'd stop changing the names. It gets confusing. Anyway, Buddy would be great when he was on his meds, but if he forgot to take them and got into a high, then he'd think he didn't need them and stop taking them altogether. I think it probably works that way for schizophrenics as well. Forget your pills once, then the voices come back and they tell you not to take them. Who are you gonna listen to? Some stupid doctor or the voice in your head?''

''How old was Trish—when she died?'' I asked.

''Twenty-three, twenty-four. Something like that. Connie's twenty-four, and I'm thinking Trish was a little younger.''

''How long had she been gone this time?'' I asked.

''About a year. Edgar had her placed first in a hospital, then a halfway house. She ran away from the halfway house about five or six months ago. He'd been searching for her—even hired private detectives, but had no idea where she was until her body turned up.''

''Poor guy,'' I said.

''He's devastated,'' Liz said. ''We went to the funeral yesterday. Edgar could barely stand up.''

''His only child?'' I asked.

Liz nodded.

''Rough,'' I said.

''Edgar's a self-made man. An orphan by the time he was twelve. Did everything the hard way. I think he thought he was used to tragedy, but then the cycle started again with Madge.'' Liz shook her head. ''I worry about him.''

''How's Mona holding up?'' I asked.

Liz gave a snort. ''As well as can be expected,'' she said. ''But if you want background on Trish, Connie would be the one to speak to.''

''Where's she living now?'' I asked, having lost track of Liz's various offspring.

''In Codderville. Didn't you get the invitation to the wedding a couple of years ago?''

Oh, great, now I felt guilty. I must have gotten it, put it aside to send a present later, and never got around to it. ''Um . . .'' I said.

Liz grinned. ''It's okay, E.J., I think you sent a casserole dish.''

I sighed relief. ''Good,'' I said.

''What I meant was: She married Garrison McLean and moved back to Codderville.''

''McLean? No kidding! I didn't realize—''

''Or you would have actually shown up for the wedding?'' Liz teased.

''Don't start,'' I said, grinning back.

Garrison McLean was the liberal Democratic state legislator from Codderville. That he was liberal was a well-kept secret, but there were enough Yellow Dog Democrats left in our part of the state to get him elected.

''Let me get you her phone number,'' Liz said, getting up to find a piece of paper to write on. ''Call her. She can tell you a lot more than I can about poor little Trish.''

I thanked Liz for the information, not so reluctantly took a couple of the kolaches she ''forced'' upon me, and left.

I drove home from Liz's house at first thinking how well I was doing. Then I stopped myself. What *was* I doing? *What* had I actually learned? That Trish Glancy had a wicked stepmother, an indulgent yet ineffectual father, a dead mom, and schizophrenia. Half of that I already knew.

Well, it's obvious, I told myself. *The wicked stepmother did it. Now all I have to do is prove it. Yeah, right,* I answered myself. I had no business messing in this. I knew it. Liz probably knew it. The wicked stepmother would definitely agree. Not to mention my wicked mother-in-law. She'd be the first one on the "drop it" bandwagon.

I had enough problems in my life without inventing a few more. I was still dealing with an angry Vera, as far as I knew Juney had dropped off the face of the earth, my three children were not improving with age, and Brenna was graduating in two weeks and I still didn't know what to get her.

Somehow, none of that stopped me from taking the turn out of Black Cat Ridge and heading for Codderville. Nor did it stop me from using my cell phone to call and ask for an emergency meeting with Anne Comstock, our family therapist. I needed more information and Anne was a font of information when it came to mental illness. Through Anne I hoped I could learn more about Trish Glancy and her illness.

The receptionist, used to my "emergency" calls, worked me in to see Anne for half an hour if I could get there in four minutes. The usual ten-minute drive to Codderville took me five, thereby giving me only twenty-nine minutes of Anne's time, but I figured I could cope.

The receptionist led me into Anne's office and offered me coffee. Thinking of the time that would take, I declined. She closed the door, and Anne immediately asked, "Is it the kids?"

I shook my head no and explained the situation,

telling her everything I knew about Juney, Trish Glancy, her murder, and her infamous stepmother as quickly and succinctly as I could.

Anne leaned back, her arms crossing her chest, and looked at me. I counted one precious minute pass. Finally, she said, "Why do you think you get involved in these things, E.J.?"

"Pardon?" I said.

"What is it you get out of involving yourself in other people's tragedies? Why do you feel you can't leave these things to the police?"

"Ah . . . I'm just trying to help people," I said, defensively. "I mean, I don't want to get involved, but when I see injustice—"

Anne actually laughed.

"What?" I demanded.

"After all the work we've done together, E.J., I would hope you could be a little more introspective than that."

I heaved a great sigh. "I like it," I said simply.

Anne nodded.

"I'm good at it," I said.

Again, she nodded.

"And I like the rush."

Anne grinned. "Now we're getting somewhere," she said.

"Not somewhere I particularly want to go, however," I said. "Willis has accused me on more than one occasion of being a danger junkie, and that's not true—"

Anne lifted an eyebrow.

"I swear that is not true!" I said. "It's the figuring

it out. The puzzle. And the fact that I can one-up my neighbor occasionally.''

''Your neighbor or the Codderville Police Department?'' Anne asked.

I shrugged. ''They're one in the same.''

''But when you do this, you're not just one-upping Elena Luna,'' Anne said. ''You're also showing up the entire force, including the chief. How does this make you feel?''

I sighed again. ''Anne, that's not why I'm here—''

''Does it make you uncomfortable to talk about your feelings in regard to this issue?''

''Of course not, but we only have thirty minutes, and I have questions I need to ask—''

''How do you think it makes me feel for you to use me as your information-gathering service?''

I leaned back in my chair, taken aback. ''What?''

''Have you thought about that?''

''I'm not sure I understand—''

''I'm a psychotherapist, E.J. Not a library. I believe we've been doing good work together, you and your family and me. But I feel you take advantage of our working relationship.''

I felt tears stinging me behind my eyes. I've never taken criticism well—not a good trait in a writer—and I felt almost betrayed by Anne's words. And, even more than betrayal, I felt like a bad girl. I was being scolded. I didn't like that. I took a deep breath and said as much.

Anne nodded. ''I understand that,'' she said.

''I guess I thought we were a team on this,'' I said. ''But you aren't really involved, are you? I didn't mean to take advantage, Anne.''

Anne nodded again. "What is it specifically you wanted to know this time?" she asked.

I shook my head and stood up. "That's okay. I'm sorry I took up your time—"

Anne pointed with her arm at the bookshelves behind her. "I have books," she said. "What's the subject?"

"Schizophrenia," I said.

She swiveled in her chair, rummaged through her books, and handed me one. "This is a guide for families with schizophrenic members. So much of the information is in laymen's terms. Bring it back next visit, okay?"

I nodded and moved toward the door.

"Are we all right, E.J.?" Anne asked.

"Are we talking the royal 'we,' the medical 'we,' or the us 'we'?"

"Us," she said.

"I'm a little embarrassed and hurt, I think," I said, trying to be honest with my feelings.

Anne smiled. "Me too. How about lunch next week, just the two of us?"

"I'll call you," I said, and headed out the door.

When I got home I found carpenters busily tearing down the back of my house. Not only were they gleefully destroying my property, they had left the gate open and Puddin' had escaped.

This was one of Puddin's many joys in life—getting out and causing havoc among the neighborhood garbage cans and cat population.

The only cats not terrified of our strange-looking animal were the trio of cats who called the Pugh house home—namely Bert, Ernie, and Axl Rose. (Guess who named the third?) Graham had been busy for the last three years training Axl Rose to be a killer attack cat. And the training was working well, unless you came up on his left side—where he was missing an eye. Bert and Ernie were very good about always approaching from the left, but Puddin' was still just a pup and, just as she hadn't learned to tell time or her ABCs as yet, she still couldn't tell her right from her left. This led to an interesting home environment.

Axl Rose did not like Puddin'. Of course, we'd yet to find anything—other than Graham and raw meat—that Axl Rose did like. Basically, if Axl Rose could figure out a way to keep Puddin' in his food bowl, he'd definitely have her for lunch.

I ascertained that the carpenters tearing down my house were actually the ones hired, then set off in the van in search of the dog. Two blocks later I saw her cavorting in someone's activated automatic sprinklers. *Great,* I thought, *I get to travel with wet dog*. There's only one thing Puddin' likes better than terrorizing the neighborhood, and that's riding in the van. I pulled up alongside her, opened the back door, and called her name. She looked up, grinned from ear to ear, shook herself, and jumped in the car. Where she, of course, shook herself again. Water sprayed the seats, the ceiling, the floor, and me. Not necessarily in that order.

If you have never seen a cross between a rottweiler and a bassett hound, let me enlighten you: They are strange-looking creatures. At least Puddin' is. She has a definite rottweiler snout and face, bassett hound ears, a long, squat body with her mother's rottweiler markings. At a year, she's mostly full-grown and about the size of a border collie—with feet the size of frying pans. When I first saw those feet when she was a puppy, I was terrified we were getting the hound from hell, but basically she just has unruly and unseemly big feet.

We drove back to the house, where I would have normally either left her in the yard to dry naturally or towel-dried her in the utility room. Since there were six men in the backyard and a large hole in the wall of the utility room, I had to take her in the front door, trying to hold her collar to keep her off the carpet while vainly trying to get her upstairs where there might, just might, be a towel.

It didn't work.

She got away from me and began rolling with glee on the living-room carpet. *That's the remodeling we should be doing,* I thought. *Tear up the carpet and just paint the cement slab!*

The cacophony of noise coming from the back of the house was a nerve-jingling terror—the fingernails-on-a-blackboard screech of nails being removed from wood, the migraine-producing thump of sledgehammers on siding, the crash and tinkle of things I didn't want to know about. I went into the living room and turned on the TV to a channel we don't get. The white noise helped drown out some of it, although the reverberating "thump-crash-screech" in the lower decibels was unerasable.

My office was off the kitchen—there was no way I could work. Maybe I could get Willis to help me move my computer upstairs to our room for the duration. Thus leaving all these workmen free to roam the downstairs portion of my home.

Okay, maybe not the greatest idea I ever had. Of course, if we had a general contractor . . .

I ventured into the kitchen to take something out of the freezer for dinner, then thought, since this was all Willis's idea in the first place, he could stop and get a pizza on his way home.

Puddin' was growling at the door to the utility room—ready to turn those workmen into Spam if she got half a chance—or lick them to death, which was most likely. The cats were gone. With any luck, maybe forever. I grabbed some cotton balls from the downstairs bath and settled into an easy chair in the living room. I stuffed the cotton in my ears. All it did was drown out the white noise.

All in all, I was not having a great day.

The book Anne had lent me was on the coffee table. I was going to have to deal with the feelings Anne's comments had aroused, but later. I picked up the book and began reading.

Basically, I discovered that schizophrenia is a severe disturbance of the brain's functioning. Okay, fine. This much I knew. The causes included changes in the chemistry of the brain, changes in the structure of the brain, genetic factors, viral infections, and head injuries. That I didn't know. Head injuries?

Neurotransmitters, chemicals released by the branches of brain cells, carry messages from the end of one nerve branch to the cell body of another. In the schizophrenic brain, something goes wrong in this communication system.

According to the book and what Liz Jones had

told me, it appeared that Trish Glancy may have suffered from gradual-onset or insidious schizophrenia, which meant a development so gradual that family and even the person with the disease may not realize that anything is wrong for a long time. And she may have been suffering from chronic schizophrenia when she died. Chronic was described in the book as a severe, long-lasting disability characterized by social withdrawal, lack of motivation, depression, blunted feelings, hallucinations, delusions, and thought disorder.

Auditory hallucinations were the most common form, according to the book. Liz Jones had definitely said something about Trish and her voices. Delusions, lack of motivation or apathy, and blunted affect were symptoms I had not heard associated with Trish Glancy—yet.

The book also gave a list of early-warning signs. I read and reread this, trying to memorize every one. There's so much to fear when you raise children—now I just added a new one—the great fear of schizophrenia, that robber of reason sneaking up on one of my kids in the years to come.

I shivered and put the book down.

I was beginning to put a face on Trish Glancy, and it made me sad. She had been a real person, with a family, a history, and a terrible disease. She wasn't just a homeless woman found murdered in the woods. She, like everyone else out there, had been a human being, with all the rights and privileges that entails.

Which, when push comes to shove, doesn't mean squat.

Six

The carpenters left at four and, when Willis got home to a silent house—as silent as a house with three unruly children can be—he couldn't understand my need for store-bought pizza.

I just looked at him. "Don't start," I said.

"What?" he asked, Mr. Innocence personified.

"Call and order a pizza, and I won't hurt you."

He rolled his eyes—man's only defense against the injustices of woman—and grabbed the phone.

The cats came strolling back later that night, and I fed and loved them—at least Bert and Ernie. Axl Rose isn't into petting.

When Willis and I crawled into bed later, I told him what I'd learned that day about Trish Glancy.

"What are you doing?" he asked.

"What?"

"E.J.!"

"What?"

He threw his book down and sat up in bed. "Don't get mixed up in this," he said, his teeth clenched.

"Mixed up in what? I just had coffee with Liz Jones, and she was telling me—"

"When was the last time you 'just had coffee with Liz Jones'?" my husband demanded.

"Willis, all I'm saying is that it's more than likely the wicked stepmother did this than poor Juney—"

"Poor Juney? Poor Juney?"

He picked up his book, looked at it, then threw it deliberately across the room, where it banged against the wall.

"We tell the children to respect books," I said to him.

"Don't go there," he said.

"Well, I'm just saying—"

"E.J."

I looked at him. My husband's a very good-looking man, but he doesn't have a sexy scowl. Some men do, but not Willis. Therefore, he was not at his sexiest at the moment.

"What?" I asked, my eyes wide.

"Stay out of this," he said.

I sighed. "I'm not doing anything!" I protested. "Liz just told me some stuff and—"

"Because you asked her. Because you went out of your way to find out that the Glancys lived next door to Liz and then you went out of your way to call Liz and get invited over for coffee, then you drove over there, then you asked her. Am I right?"

"About what?"

He got up and retrieved his book. "I'm not speaking to you anymore," he said. He stuck his nose back in his book.

"Honey," I said.

"Hum da hum da," Willis said, wetting his finger and turning a page.

"Baby," I said.

"La de la la la."

I kissed his right nipple. He batted at my nose. I ran my tongue along the line of hair that goes from his breastbone to his belly button.

Willis put down the book.

Tuesday I decided it was time to make up with Vera. The carpenters were there, and, since there was a hole in the wall the size of Dallas, I decided it didn't make any difference who stole all our stuff—the carpenters or the hordes of thieves that could just walk in through the hole. And I had no desire to stay in my home. I put Puddin' on her leash, and the two of us got in the van and headed for Codderville.

I knocked on Vera's back door and opened it. She didn't believe in locking her doors except at night—and we'd had to convince her of that—so this was generally my method of entrance. Go to the back door, knock once, and open the door, yelling "Vera" as I did so.

She was standing at the stove in the kitchen. She turned and looked at me. "Well," she said.

"Hey," I said.

Garth was sitting at the kitchen table with a coloring book. On seeing me, he said, "Auntie E.J.!" and jumped down, running up to hug me. I grabbed him up and swung him in the air. We both giggled. I kissed his nose. "How's my fella?" I asked.

"Fine," he said. "How's *my* fella?"

"Fine," I said.

He patted my face. "You're delicious!" he said.

I laughed and set him down. "What's Granma fixing?" I asked.

"Food," Garth said. A succinct answer if ever there was one.

"Dinner," came Vera's reply.

"Smells good," I said.

"Don't suck up," Vera said. "It doesn't become you."

"I'm just trying to make nice," I said.

"Well, you can make nice till you're blue in the face, but I know betrayal when I see it. Read your Bible much, E.J.? Story of Judas ring any bells? Did you get your thirty pieces of silver?"

"Vera, I think you're overreacting—"

I knew as the words were coming out of my mouth that they weren't the ones I should be saying. She turned off the burner under her dinner, picked Garth up in one arm, and headed for her bedroom, slamming doors behind her. While I got a quick burst of déjà vu.

I checked the contents of the pot on the stove. Vera had regressed to the old country ways when Garth came to live with her. Dinner was at the noon hour, supper was at night. There was a very nice stew in the pot—lots of hunks of beef, pearl onions, baby carrots, new potatoes, in a good thick beef gravy. It smelled delicious.

I turned the burner on low, found a tomato ripening on the windowsill, sliced that and some cucumber from the crisper in the fridge, set the table for three, poured milk for Garth and iced tea for Vera and myself, and went down the hall to the closed door of her bedroom.

I tapped lightly. "Dinner's ready," I sang out. "Last one to the table gets gristle!"

I went back into the kitchen. Garth ran in and climbed up in his chair, Vera not far behind him. "There is *no* gristle in my stew!" she said.

I brought the pot to the table and ladled stew onto Garth's plate, saying, "Be careful, honey, it's hot." Then I ladled some onto Vera's plate. "Looks and smells delicious," I said.

"You're sucking up again," she said.

"Fat lot of good it's doing me, too," I said, sitting down to my own steaming plate.

Vera glared at me as she stuffed her face.

I said, "I found out some stuff about the murder victim."

Vera said nothing.

I said nothing.

Garth said, "What's a murder vitim?"

"Victim," I said. "It's police talk," I told him.

Garth's eyes got big. "Are you a policeman, Auntie E.J.?"

"No, but if I were, I'd be a police officer, because police officers can be both men and women."

"So if you're not a policeman, how come you talk police talk?" Garth said.

"Because my next-door neighbor—a lady—is a police *officer*," I stressed. This is not the conversation I'd planned on.

"And she taught you to talk police talk?" Garth asked.

"Um-hum, now eat your stew," I said.

"Talk some more of it, Auntie E.J.," he said.

"APB," I said.

"Perp," Vera said.

"Miranda rights," I said.

"Scumbag," Vera said.

"Freeze or I'll shoot, scumbag!" Garth said, his little hands clasped together in front of him, index fingers pointed like a gun.

Vera giggled.

"You're letting him watch 'Hill Street' reruns, aren't you?" I asked.

"Garth, baby, finish up. Granma and Aunt E.J. gotta talk, honey," Vera said. "You go in my room and play with your toys."

"I wanna talk more police talk!" Garth wailed.

"Tell you what," I said, bending toward him, "next time you're at my house, I'll take you next door to meet my neighbor, okay?"

"The policeman lady?" Garth asked.

"The police officer, yes," I said.

"Okay," he said, jumping down from his chair and heading for Vera's bedroom.

Vera looked at me, one eyebrow raised. "So?" she said.

"So what?" I replied.

She sighed. One of those patented Pugh sighs that only she and her surviving son manage to accomplish. "Tell me about the 'vitim,' " she said.

I told her all I'd learned about Trish Glancy, her wicked stepmother and ineffectual father.

"Crazy, huh?" Vera said as she began picking up the plates from the table. "I'm not surprised. All homeless people are crazy is what I heard."

I sighed. It may not be a genuine Pugh sigh, but I've lived among these people long enough to learn something. "Vera, that's not true. As usual, you know very little about the subject."

"Oh, really?" she said, fighting me for my plate as I stood up to help clean off the table. I'm bigger. I won.

"Yeah, really. Where do you get your information, anyway? The supermarket checkout line?"

"Don't you start with me," she said, grabbing the plate out of my hand. "You're always starting with me!"

"I'm sorry, you're right."

"Ha!" she said.

"But, and here are some facts I looked up on the internet—"

"Oh, well that's gospel," my mother-in-law muttered.

"Three percent of the American population is homeless—"

"That's a lot of crazy people—" Vera started.

"Dammit, Vera!"

She glared at me. "You don't have to get vulgar," she said.

"About a quarter or less of the homeless population are mentally ill. And about a quarter do drugs—"

"Well, that's half!"

"But those quarters overlap. A lot of the mentally ill are drug abusers, and vice versa—"

"And this is good news?"

"Which means that half to three-quarters of the people out there living on the streets are 'normal'! They work, either full- or part-time! Do you know what minimum wage in this country is, Vera? Do you know how much even an apartment in a bad neighborhood costs? There are people out there working their asses off and taking showers at the bus station because they have to live in their cars! The fastest-growing group are families with children! Normal people, Vera! Victims of downsizing, and layoffs, and just plain bad luck!" I took a breath. "So get your facts straight before you go off on a tangent!"

Very calmly, my mother-in-law said, "So who's going off on a tangent? Only tangent going on around here is coming from you, I do believe."

"All I'm saying is—" I started.

"Is that I'm a prejudiced old ninny who's always making vast generalizations."

I shrugged. "Well, I don't know about prejudiced or ninny, but you do tend to generalize."

Vera sighed. Hands on hips, she said, "Okay. I don't like Juney. I've never liked Juney. I figure if she's homeless, it's because she deserves it! That's not a generalization, honey, that's real personal!"

"Do you really, truly, deep in your heart think she could have killed that woman, Vera?"

She turned away from me, staring out the window. Finally, she said, "No. I guess not. She's stupid and she's lazy and she's selfish. But I don't think she's mean."

"Okay—" I started.

"But it coulda been a dumb accident," she said, her look hopeful. "That I wouldn't put past her at all. Wouldn't be the first time she killed somebody through a dumb accident."

"Vera, she wasn't driving—"

"Don't," she said, her face creasing with age right in front of me. "I won't talk about that."

I nodded. "This wasn't a dumb accident," I said. "Someone beat Trish Glancy's head in with a blunt object. No accident about that."

Vera sat down at the table. "Maybe she tripped—"

I shook my head.

"Maybe Juney dropped something on her."

Again I shook my head.

Vera sighed. "Well, she is Garth's mother," she said.

I nodded.

"Wouldn't be right for the boy to grow up thinking his mama killed somebody. Specially if she didn't do it."

I nodded.

Again, the sigh. This time appearing to come all the way from her toes. "I guess we'd better find her," Vera said.

I leaned down and hugged her. After a minute, she hugged me back.

"Your mother wants me to find Juney," I told my husband at dinner. The entire family was at the table—dog at Megan's feet, cats staring at us from the kitchen floor. I thought it would be best to say what I had to say in front of the children. Willis would try not to go entirely ballistic in front of the children.

"She does?" he said, calmly reaching for the bowl of broccoli on the table.

"Uh-huh," I said, taking a bite of chicken.

"That's nice," he said, spooning broccoli onto his plate.

Which to an outsider would have seemed like a normal, everyday thing to do. To an outsider, this would seem as if Willis were as calm as a placid pond. If the outsider didn't know that my husband hated broccoli and would never, ever put the evil green anywhere near his plate if he were in his right mind.

"I said I'd do what I could," I told him.

"I'm sure Mother's pleased," he said. He actually took a bite of the vegetable.

"She appears to be," I said.

He spit the broccoli back on his plate. His taste buds must have been more alert than the rest of him.

My children, whose idea of funny is anything to do with farting, puking, or spitting, thought this hysterical.

Willis stood up. "I'm going to bed," he said, and walked out the back door.

I told the kids to be quiet and eat, and followed my husband into the backyard.

The carpenters had knocked down part of the fence while trying to get their equipment into the backyard. There were piles of lumber and assorted manly things dumped haphazardly around the yard. I was barefoot, which is not a sensible position to be in when there are nails and other objects of pain lying about.

"Okay," I said to Willis's back, "let it out."

He turned. He shook his head. He gave me his back.

"Honey—"

"You and my mother." He shook his head. "You and my mother."

"Isn't it better now that we get along?" I said, trying for a light tone.

"No," he said. "No, it definitely isn't."

"Honey, this is better," I said.

He turned and looked at me. "Maybe I just miss the way it used to be—me and you against the world," he said, his voice soft.

I smiled. "It still is. Always will be."

He touched my face softly and shook his head. "No. It hasn't been that way in a long time. And it will never be that way again."

"Willis—"

He leaned down slightly and kissed me. "Sometimes I miss the way we used to be," he said. "Before—" He pointed abstractedly toward the house. "All of that," he said.

I curled into his arms. "I know," I said. "Ain't growing up a bitch?"

He laughed softly into the starry night and hugged me tighter. "I want to go back fifteen years. I want to be alone with you in Mexico, with Daddy still alive and Dusty causing them hell. And no Juney. No Juney at all."

I took his face in my hands. "And no Graham, and no Megan, and no Bessie. And without a Juney, there would never be a Garth. And we'd still be making ten dollars and fifty cents an hour and thinking we were rich while we tried to save up enough money for a battery for the VW bus.''

''And we'd get high on the weekends and tool around the ruins and run into people we'd get tight with and never see again,'' he said.

''And worry about which one of them was a narc,'' I said.

''Remember OD Debbie?'' he said, a glint of mischief in his eyes.

''And Trippy Max?'' I said.

''And Q Boy and Red Fred?''

I looked my husband in the eye. ''Would you really want to be around those people again?''

Willis sighed. ''Not for a single second,'' he said, and kissed me. ''But I would like—just for a little while—not to worry so goddamn much.''

I wrapped my arms around his waist. ''Then don't,'' I said. ''Just stop it. We've got money in the bank, we have health insurance, and we've got three terrific, healthy—although weird—kids. What's to worry?''

''I don't want you running around trying to find a murderer,'' he said.

''What murderer? I'm trying to find Juney!''

''Exactly.''

''Willis, your mother and I both agree Juney's not the murderer.''

''That's because you and my mother both agree you don't *want* Juney to be the murderer. Wanting it doesn't make it so, Eej.''

''Do you think Juney could have done this?'' I asked him.

He shook his head. ''I have no idea. I don't know

her. And neither do you. Neither does my mother. We don't know this woman, E.J. She was married to my brother for five minutes and he knocked her up. Her son is my brother's seed. That's all we know. That's it."

"I don't believe she did it, Willis. But if she did, then I want to know why. Garth is going to deserve to know at least that, don't you think?"

Willis sighed. "Next year," he said. "A desert island. Just you and me and the kids. And Puddin'. And maybe the cats."

"And your mother—"

"Okay, but that's all—"

"And Garth—"

"We're not bringing Luna—"

"Well, her boys at least. The kids will need someone to play with—"

Willis backed me up to the fence, my arms stretched high above me, his hands pinning my wrists. "Okay, at least a motel room with nobody else for forty-eight hours," he said.

"Deal," I said.

Then the back door opened and our life got back to normal.

Seven

The next morning I took the kids to school, then drove to Codderville to Vera's. Then the two of us took Garth to "mother's day out" at Vera's church, and headed to the only homeless shelter in Codder County.

I wasn't thrilled about having Vera with me, but she had insisted. With my mother-in-law, it is best to do what she wants when she wants. Life is easier that way. Less painful. I had this horrible image, however, of walking into the shelter and seeing Vera making faces as if she smelled something foul.

Luckily, she surprised me. Vera's political views might be out of the Dark Ages, but being a card-carrying Baptist she knows a thing or two about charity. Before we left, she'd signed her Sunday school class up to ladle soup on Monday nights.

The shelter was housed in a defunct grocery store in a section of town that had never taken off. The housing project that had been planned for the area went belly up after the supermarket and a strip center had been built. Now the storefronts of the strip center sported signs for marginal businesses like MADAM REYNA READER & ADVISER, LILI ANN'S HAIR BRAIDING N' NAIL SALON, THE CRYSTAL CITY NEW AGE HEALTH & BOOK BOUTIQUE, and a store with no name but garishly tie-dyed T-shirts filling the window space.

The defunct supermarket was the major space in the strip center. We parked in the huge, practically empty parking lot and went in the doors of the center. The automatic doors of the supermarket were still working. A group of men stood a few feet from the entrance, smoking and looking at us furtively. They, like Trish Glancy and my sister-in-law, were wearing too many layers of clothes for the weather. Several had backpacks or duffel bags. The two white men in the group were sun-baked an unhealthy brown, what hair they had peeking out from under frayed fishermen hats dirty and sun-dried. A very dark African-American man, dressed in crusty layers, leaned heavily on a crutch, one leg missing from the knee down.

I felt Vera stiffen beside me, and I hurried her inside the shelter.

The huge space had been partitioned off, so that what we first walked into was a small office/foyer with walls that went up about ten feet, stopping short of the high, open-duct ceiling. A woman of undetermined age sat at a rickety card table on a folding chair. She had gray hair, an unlined face, and a huge chest. She smiled at us as we walked in.

"May I help you?" she said.

"We're looking—" started Vera.

I interrupted. "Hi, I'm E.J. Pugh and this is my mother-in-law, Vera Pugh." I held my hand out to the woman, who shook it with a hand as damp and limp as a dead fish.

"Marty Everston," she said, holding her hand out to Vera, who took it proudly and shook—as if she had never made the statement in my presence that women shaking hands was only for bra-burners. I know, I know, an antiquated term, but this is Vera we're dealing with here.

"What can I do for you?" Ms. Everston said, standing.

"We have reason to believe that a family member might be staying here," I said. "And of course, if she is, we want to bring her home."

The woman nodded, but the smile faded. "Sometimes," she said, "people come here in spite of the fact that they have family. We try to maintain the privacy of our clients. I hope you can understand that."

"Of course," I said. "All we want to do is to make sure she knows she can come home. She has a little boy who misses her terribly."

Vera kicked my shin at this comment.

"All I can do is take your name and number, and if this person wants to contact you, she can," Ms. Everston said.

I wrote down both my name and Vera's and both our phone numbers. Then I wrote down the only name I knew for my sister-in-law, Juney Trublood Pugh, and gave Ms. Everston the only picture we had—a five-year-old picture of a seventeen-year-old Juney about six months pregnant.

Ms. Everston looked at the picture and shook her head. "Sorry. I can truthfully tell you I've never seen this woman, and I don't know the name."

"She's older now," I said. "About twenty-three. And not pregnant. Very skinny, in fact."

The woman continued to shake her head. "Nope," she said, handing me back the picture. "Haven't seen her, and I have a good memory for faces."

I pushed the picture back. "Keep it," I said. "In case she comes in?"

Ms. Everston nodded her head. "I'll do what I can," she said, "but we're awfully busy here with so little help."

Ah, the commercial, I thought.

Which was the point where Vera and Marty Everston started negotiating for Vera's Sunday school class. I hoped the little old ladies in her group would be as thrilled about the prospect as Vera appeared to be.

"Let me show you around," Marty Everston said. "We keep a tight ship around here."

She led us to a door on the left, which led into a large dining room filled tightly with long tables with connecting benches. They were old and scarred and looked like they might have come from a renovated high-school cafeteria. It was still a little early for lunch, but several people—mostly women but a few men—were stationed behind the cafeteria-style serving area, stirring food, arranging plastic plates and utensils, and generally getting ready for the noon rush.

An accordian-pleated room divider separated the dining room from the sleeping quarters beyond.

"We can open this up in the wintertime if it freezes and just let people sleep on the floor."

Vera shook her head.

"It's better than outside," Marty Everston said.

"Amen," my mother-in-law said.

"How many beds?" I asked.

"We can accommodate fifty men in this area and on the other side of the entrance is the dorm for women and children. We can take twenty-five there."

"I understand women and children are becoming the new poor—how come more accommodations for men than women?" I asked.

"Because this was set up when nobody knew those statistics," she said. "Most shelters are set up to accommodate more men. That's why a lot of women with kids will lie and say they're battered so they can get in a battered women's shelter for a little while."

I hugged my arms to myself, trying not to say anything. Marty smiled at me. "I know, believe me. But the slowest thing in the world to change is social service. We're at the bottom of the totem pole as far as most politicians go; so we're the last to get money, change, anything. But we're always the first to get cut."

"What can I do to help?" I asked.

"Write your congressperson, volunteer for Habitat for Humanity, or"—and here she grinned—"write me a check. We take donations."

I got my checkbook out. A healthy balance and a worthy cause have always been my downfall.

* * *

Upon leaving the shelter, one of the men leaning against the building approached us.

"Got any spare change?" he asked.

Vera stopped and looked at him. "No, I don't. But if you wait here, I'll go home and make you a sandwich," she said.

"Hell, mama, 'fore you got back here with it, the kitchen'll be open."

"You mow lawns?" she asked.

"You got a lawn mower, you bet," he said.

Vera took a piece of paper out of her purse and wrote down something. "This is the address of my church. You go there and I'll call Brother Michael and tell him you're coming. The grass is getting a bit high. You do a good job, maybe some of the old ladies around there'll start using you."

He looked at the piece of paper. "How'm I supposed to get there?" he asked.

"Well, son," Vera said, "you gotta have a little initiative."

She turned and walked toward the van. I looked at the man, handed him a buck, shrugged, and followed my mother-in-law.

As we left the parking lot, we discovered that neither of us had done anything about a gift for Brenna's graduation, so we hightailed it out to the highway and the new outlet mall.

The one thing Brenna always needed was clothes. She had come to us with none of her own—just her mother's eighties rejects that were two sizes too big and ten years too old for her—not to mention cheap and out-of-date when they were purchased during the Reagan administration.

We went into one of the nicer boutiques, and I bought two outfits and purchased a nice-sized gift certificate that I made sure would be good through the summer so that Brenna could buy some things for college in the fall.

Vera was making "tsk, tsk" sounds as I checked out.

"What?" I said.

"That's what you're gonna get her?" she said. "Clothes?"

"Not all!" I said, okay defensively. "This is just a little something," I said. "What are *you* getting her?" I challenged.

Vera sighed. "I don't have the foggiest notion. She still hasn't made up her mind which school she's gonna accept, so I don't know whether to buy her an airline ticket if she goes to Northwestern, or a new car if she goes to Austin."

"Vera, you can't afford either of those things!"

She grinned. "I know. But you and Willis can."

"She's going to Austin," I said.

"Maybe—maybe not," Vera said.

"Northwestern's too far. She'll get homesick."

"Girl's got an independent streak a mile wide, E.J. Had to, the way she was raised," Vera said. "And we gotta let her make her own choice. She worked real hard for those scholarships, and you know the one from Northwestern's better than the one from UT."

"For Heaven's sake, Vera. This is a small-town girl! In Chicago?" I demanded.

Vera patted my arm. "Honey, you got to learn to let go."

We picked up Garth from "mother's day out," and I dropped the two of them at Vera's, ostensibly heading for home. But it was still early. If I went home all I could do would be work—and I had an aversion to even turning on my computer these days. Once I turned it on, I would actually do some work on my latest romance, but it was remarkable the things I could do to keep my finger from actually touching that button that turned the dreaded machine on.

I knew this aversion had something to do with the $85,000 check we'd gotten from Bessie's grandmother's estate. I wrote romances for gravy money—a vacation every three or four years, emergency car repairs and dental work, and the like. That need would easily be filled now for some time to come. I didn't *have* to turn on the computer. It was no longer a necessity.

I turned into a parking lot and got my cell phone out of my purse and the number for daughter Connie that Liz Jones had given me. I called the number, and Connie picked up on the third ring.

"Hello?"

"Hi, Connie?"

"Yes?"

"You probably don't remember me. My name's E.J. Pugh, I'm a friend of your mom's—"

"Oh, E.J., hi! Mom said you might be calling! It's about poor Trish, right?"

"Right. I'm just trying to find out what I can about

Trish. My sister-in-law appears to be the sheriff's prime suspect—''

''Yeah, Mom told me. That's just awful. Look, I'm just putting Ethan down for his nap. Could you come by here?''

''Sure,'' I said, since I'd been trying to figure out how to angle an invitation anyway. She gave me directions, and I hung up the cell phone, heading east out of Codderville.

The Codder County state representative, Mr. Garrison McLean, I had only seen on television. I'd voted for him twice, and would do it a third time—whether he ran for state rep or a higher office. Personally, I was hoping he'd try for congress. Our current congressman considered Newt Gingrich a liberal. And with the state Congress was in these days—okay, okay, I won't go there.

McLean, by his countenance on TV, was a handsome man. In his mid-thirties, almost six and a half feet tall, broad-shouldered, with straight teeth, a good smile with one killer dimple in his left cheek, and sparkling green eyes. Or at least they sparkled on TV. Yes, I paid attention to him. He's definitely a John Kennedy for the nineties, but hopefully only in his politics and looks, not in his womanizing—for Connie's sake.

I knew McLean came from a prominent family in Codder County, had been the star of his high-school basketball team, a star player at the University of Texas, and only a knee injury his senior year kept him from being drafted by the pros. He'd gone on to law school and then immediately began working for former Governor Anne Richards's campaign.

After her election, he landed a plum job in her administration and branched out into his own political career just shortly before she was beaten at the next election.

He'd been our state rep for five years. Why I didn't know he had married Liz Jones's daughter is beyond me. I guess it must have happened during one of my infrequent apolitical periods.

The house I came to by Connie's directions was a long, lean ranch-style on a large spread bordered by a white-rail fence. The house was probably thirty to forty years old, made of rock and redwood with lots of glass. A late-fifties, early-sixties modern ranch that had to have cost a bundle when it was built. It curved with the land, and it was hard to tell where it ended.

I drove up the asphalt drive to the circle in front and parked. Connie opened the front door, leaning against it with a smile on her face as I approached.

Connie was what my husband has always referred to as a "big, smelly white woman." Somehow, this is a compliment. Connie was lush. Six feet tall, big-breasted, long-limbed, she wore her clothes like they were ready to fall off. Dark honey blond hair fell haphazardly to her shoulders and beyond. Just looking at her, you knew she did nothing more than wake up, wash her face, and run a quick hand through her hair. And still, you wished you looked just like her. Go figure.

"Hey, you," she said by way of greeting. "Haven't seen you in a long time."

I walked up to the porch and she hugged me, even

though we'd probably only met twice in our lives. She was definitely Liz Jones's daughter.

"Come on in, I made strudel." Oh, definitely Liz's daughter. I could smell it from the open doorway.

The house was huge, with rooms off rooms off rooms. I followed her down a Mexican-tiled hall to a huge great room with the kitchen attached. The furniture, as would befit a family of giants, was oversize and comfortable-looking. Baby toys scattered the large hooked rug, and a golden retriever raised its head long enough to see that I was no threat before lowering it and going back to sleep in front of the fireplace.

"God, I couldn't believe it about Trish," Connie said, leading me to the kitchen table, where strudel and coffee cups were set out. "Sugar, sweetener, or black?"

"Equal?"

"Got it," she said, pouring me a cup of dark, evil-looking brew. "I mean, I guess I can believe it, that's where she was headed. But you know."

"It's rough," I said.

"God, her dad at the funeral! Jeez! It was awful."

"Do you know anyone who would want to hurt Trish?" I asked.

Connie shook her head. "Hell, I don't know anybody who even knew Trish anymore. I mean, it's not like she came to the high-school reunions or anything."

"Had you heard from her at all?"

Connie shook her head. "Funny you should ask that. I did as a matter of fact. She started calling here a couple of months ago. I really never understood what she was blathering on about. But she kept calling. We finally had to get an unlisted number, but somehow she got that, too. Garrison made me file a complaint with the sheriff's office. I don't know what they did about it, but she stopped after we changed the phone number again."

"What would she say when she called?"

Connie shrugged. "Who knows? It didn't make any sense. Trish was . . . Well, Trish was a little out of it."

"When you were kids, what was she like?"

Connie smiled. "She was great. She was my best friend. We were both kinda misfits, I guess you'd say. When you're in junior high and you're six-foot-even and a girl, you're definitely a misfit. And Trish, well she was very shy. She'd had a speech impediment when she was little, and even though that was cured, she still felt everybody was making fun of her. And they probably were. A lot of the kids at the junior high had gone to elementary school with her. And you know how rotten kids are."

"Tell me about it," I said. "I'm raising three of the rottenest."

"But I really loved Trish's mom. She was the best. She saw me one day slumping down the stairs at her house, and she said, 'Straighten up, girl. Show 'em all how beautiful you are!' I just looked at her. Right, I was thinking, I'm a real fox." Connie took a bite of strudel. "Two days later she had Trish and me both signed up for a modeling class. 'When you're in Paris being the toast of the town,' she said, 'let them laugh then!' " Connie smiled. "Mrs. Glancy was wonderful."

"And Mr. Glancy?" I asked.

Connie shrugged. "I wouldn't know. I think I saw him at Trish's house maybe three or four times in all the years we hung out. He was always working."

"I got the impression from your mother that the new Mrs. Glancy is not one of your favorite people," I said.

"Ha!" Connie said. "Mona's a pig. Believe me, *I'll* never call her Mrs. Glancy. That was Madge Glancy's name, not that bitch's."

"Trish didn't get along with her?"

"No one gets along with Mona. Ask any of the poor women who used to work in the office at Glancy Industries. There has to be a couple of thousand of them. She ran through underlings like some people do Kleenex."

"Can you think of any reason why Mona would want to . . . well . . ."

"Kill Trish?" Connie said with a small smile. "No. I wish I could tell you a thousand reasons and help you handcuff the bitch, but as long as Trish was out of her hair and out of the will, I don't think Mona gave a damn what happened to her."

"Mr. Glancy seemed to be spending a lot of time and money trying to find Trish," I said.

Connie shook her head. "He was just going through the motions. Not that I'm saying he doesn't—didn't—love Trish. I think in his way he did a lot. But his way is to hire someone to take care of the problem. Which is what he did with Trish. Hired doctors and shrinks to put her away, then hired PIs to find her when she ran away. I'm sure none of this had any effect on Mona. What little he spent trying to find his daughter, the company made back tenfold in a day. Mona's gonna be a very rich woman one of these days. Which is exactly what she's been planning since poor Mrs. Glancy was first diagnosed."

"What makes you think Trish wasn't in Mr. Glancy's will?" I asked.

Connie shrugged. "I don't. I just think at the most he would make provisions for her care—some nice hospital or halfway house. He wouldn't leave a schizophrenic several mil. He might love his daughter, but he's not stupid."

"What about boyfriends?" I asked.

Connie shook her head. "Trish never had a boyfriend that I knew of. In junior high she was crazy about this one boy, but he moved away our freshman year. In high school, after Trish's mom died and we stopped being so tight, we ran in the same crowd, and there were boys in that crowd, but Trish didn't go with any one guy. Far as I know, she was a virgin in high school. Maybe when she died."

"You know anything about what happened to her when she went off to Stanford?"

Connie shook her head. "No. I was at UT then. Mom told me when Mr. Glancy went and got her and brought her back. And that she'd been found in a homeless shelter." Connie sighed. "She started getting strange our senior year in high school. She'd just zone out sometimes. Sometimes she'd start twitching. I heard her talking to people once when no one was there. I thought she was on drugs. I still think maybe she was."

"What makes you say that?"

"There was this one boy who kinda hung on the

fringe of our group that I know was doing dope. At least reefer. I think crack, too. I saw him with a crack pipe once. Trish was tighter with him than anybody else in the group was. I don't think he would have been hanging out with us at all if it weren't for Trish."

"But you said she didn't have a boyfriend. Do you think—"

"No. Jimmy was gay. He made no bones about that."

"Do you know where he is now?" I asked.

Connie shook her head. "I went to the reunion last year and didn't see him. Not that I was exactly looking for him. Somebody said he'd moved to California."

Did he? I wondered. And if he did, had it been the same time Trish Glancy had gone to California?

"Jimmy who?" I asked.

"Jimmy Nagle." She got up from the table and left the room, coming back in just a moment with what could only be a high-school yearbook. "I had this out looking at pictures of Trish," she said wistfully. She flipped through the pages. "Here," she said, pointing to a picture of a young man in suit coat and tie. His hair was straight and over his ears, parted in the middle. A very light color in the black and white photo—probably blond. He had a prominent nose and zits on his forehead. He wasn't smiling in the picture.

Jimmy Nagle looked like about two million other boys who graduated sometime in the early nineties. He wouldn't be easy to find. If it were even necessary to do so.

"Where's Trish?" I asked.

Connie turned the pages back to the "Gs." There she was. I'd only seen Trish Glancy in death, after years of the ravages of disease and homelessness. The girl shyly smiling back at me from the pages of the Codderville High "Roarbook" bore little resemblance to the emaciated bundle of rags I'd seen in the clearing in the woods. She had dark blond hair with the high bangs that were so popular with girls in the early nineties, and seemed to be wearing too much makeup. But her smile was an orthodontist's wet dream. She had been pretty. Quietly pretty.

Connie, standing above me, reached out a long index finger and traced Trish's face. "She used to be such a good friend," Connie said. "We used to tell each other everything."

I squeezed Connie's hand. "I'm so sorry," I said.

I got up and thanked her for the strudel and coffee. Connie walked me to the door.

"Good luck with your sister-in-law," she said.

"Thanks. She's got a little boy who's going to need her," I said.

Connie nodded her head. "I understand that." Just then a yelp came from the back of the house. Connie laughed. "Speak of the devil!" she said.

"Give him a kiss for me," I said, and headed for my car.

Eight

I drove home wondering where Juney could be. Codderville and Black Cat Ridge are basically two small towns, one on each side of the Colorado River. There's a lot of country around us. She could be anywhere. How many homeless camps could there be along the banks of the Colorado? How many in abandoned buildings and vacant lots? Around railroad tracks and in farmers' back forties?

The last time I'd actually seen Juney she'd been in La Grange. That was thirty miles away. But that was before her stuff had been found at Trish Glancy's camp right outside of Codderville.

Okay, so she'd been in La Grange, then come back to Codderville. Did that mean she was still in Codderville or back in La Grange? Or Brenham? Or Houston? Or Tim-Buc-Tu?

When she'd dropped Garth off at Vera's she'd left on foot. Unless she'd had a car stashed around the corner. But when I saw her in La Grange, she'd run away from me on foot. There had been no car stashed around the corner where she'd been, for all intents and purposes, begging.

She could have gotten a ride anywhere. But something told me she hadn't. Something told me she wouldn't get that far away from Garth.

But she's deserted him before, my other self said. *Left him for a whole year!* True, but that had been different—he was a newborn infant when she left him. She hadn't bonded with him. Since then, she'd raised Garth for three years. There was a true bond there now. *Really?* my other self said. *Why?*

Because I wanted there to be. Simple as that. I wanted Juney to be more than everyone else thought she was. I wanted Dusty to have done one thing smart in his life and chosen wisely the mother of his child. I wanted Garth to have someone who truly loved him and cared for him and thought of his welfare above all else. Someone who would rather give him up than have him living on the streets.

I didn't want Garth to be Juney's burden.

But where's her other kid? my other self asked. *Remember when she came and got Garth when he was a year old? She had a husband and a bun in the oven then, remember? Where's that kid now?*

I told my other self to shut the hell up and drove to the school to pick up my kids.

After I'd gotten the kids home, snacked, and in their rooms bitching because they couldn't go in the backyard due to the construction, I called Luna at the station.

"Luna," she said.

"Any word on my sister-in-law?" I asked.

"No."

"Anything new on Trish Glancy?" I asked.

"No."

"Anything at all you want to tell me?" I asked.

"No."

"Luna, I can't tell you how much I appreciate the confidences you share with me. It means so much."

"Goodbye," she said.

Well, so much for my close liaison with the Codderville Police Department.

I didn't know where to look or what to do. I kept reminding myself it wasn't any of my business anyway, but that didn't seem to do any good. A woman I didn't know was dead, and a woman I barely knew may have done it. Basically, there was no connection to me. None whatsoever. But then I'd remember the little face of Garth Dustin Pugh, remember that summer in Mexico with Dusty, and knew I did owe Juney something. I owed her my concern, my caring, and my busybody nose. I'd done it for the Lesters, for myself, for my husband, for Brenna. Now it was time to do it for my little dead brother-in-law and the child he never knew.

And the woman they both loved. Whoever the hell she was.

I called Vera. I couldn't remember Juney's mother's last name. It hadn't been the same as Juney's because she'd remarried. I didn't for a minute think

Juney would be there, but there was an outside chance the woman might know where her daughter was.

"Juney's mother?" Vera repeated when I asked my question. "Lord, why would you want to talk to that woman?"

"There's an outside chance she might know where Juney is," I explained.

"Ha," said my mother-in-law. "Well, I know her first name was Loretta and that piece of filth she was married to was named Tom. Let me think now." There was silence on the other end of the line while Vera thought. "Mason? Madison? Moreland!" she shouted, just like a hallelujah in her church. "Tom and Loretta Moreland," she said. "Scum of the earth."

"Garth's other grandparents."

"That don't make 'em decent," Vera said, and hung up.

I looked up Tom Moreland in the Greater Codderville/Black Cat Ridge phone book. There was only one. Actually, there's only one John Smith, too. We're a small area.

A woman's voice answered on the second ring. "Hello?"

"Mrs. Moreland?" I asked. "Loretta Moreland?"

"Who's this?" she asked, her voice instantly suspicious.

"Is this Loretta Moreland?"

"Who wants to know?"

I sighed. This was going to be fun. "This is E.J. Pugh. I'm Juney's sister-in-law."

"What's that to me?"

"I'm trying to get in touch with Juney."

"Fine. And if you do, tell the little tramp not to come 'round here no more." Mrs. Moreland hung up in my ear.

The "no more" seemed to indicate to me that Juney may have dropped by. I hit redial.

"What?" came the rude response.

"Please don't hang up, Mrs. Moreland. Has Juney been by to see you?"

"What if she has?"

"Could you tell me when this was?"

"You the police?" she demanded.

"No, I'm Juney's sister—"

"Then I don't got to tell you squat." She hung up again.

Lovely woman, I thought.

I called Luna back. After she answered I said, "I just talked to Loretta Moreland, Juney's—"

"Mother. Yeah, I know."

"You know she's Juney's mother or you know I talked to her?" I asked.

"I know she's Juney's mother! So what?"

"According to her, Juney's been by there to see her."

"I know."

I was silent. "You know?" I demanded. "Then why didn't you tell me?"

"Why *would* I tell you, Pugh? This is a police investigation. I *do not* have to check in with you."

"It would be the polite thing to do," I said icily.

"I'm not in the business of being polite," shc said.

"No shit," I said.

"Goodbye," she said.

''Wait!'' I yelled.

''What?''

''When did she go by her mother's house?'' I asked.

There was silence.

''Please, Luna. We're worried about her. Her little boy is worried about her.''

Luna sighed. ''Before she ever came by Vera's, looks like,'' she said. ''According to the mother—who is a real piece of work, by the way—''

''I noticed—''

''She came by and tried to drop off the kid, but dear Loretta wasn't having any of it and basically told Juney to hit the road. According to her, she didn't even let her in the door.''

''I'm not noticeably surprised,'' I said.

''That's all I've got.''

''Right,'' I said.

''I'm not kidding,'' she said.

''You would never kid me,'' I agreed. ''You'd lie to me, but you'd never kid me.''

''Bye, Pugh.'' Another woman hung up in my ear. I was beginning to feel a little rejected.

I tried to think what else I could do. I knew there had to be something. Then I remembered the high-school druggie from Trish's past. I'd written the name down when I'd gotten back in the van after leaving Connie. I went out to the van to look for it.

You'd think as a writer that I would have little notebooks or possibly small tape recorders in likely spots like my office, my bedside table, next to the bathtub, and, of course, in the van. That would make entirely too much sense. I write things down on whatever's handy: the backs of envelopes, used sticky pads, and body parts when I'm desperate. I found a crumpled receipt from the grocery store on the floor of the front passenger seat of the van. I smoothed it out, turned it over and—*voilà!* There it was: Jimmy Nagel.

I took the note back into the kitchen, where I almost ran into a carpenter drinking straight from the tap of my sink.

"Would you like a glass for that?" I asked.

"Don't want to put you out none," he said.

I found a plastic pitcher and some paper cups, filled the pitcher up with ice and water and handed it to him. "Share," I said.

He grinned and went back through the hole in the utility room.

I took the cordless phone and the phone book into the living room so I could be a little farther away from the sound of nail guns, and looked under "N" for Nagel. There were two: Robert J. Nagel and a B. Nagel, which meant it was probably a woman. I tried Robert J.'s number first.

A woman answered on the first ring, as if she'd been sitting on the phone. Her voice whispered a tentative "Hello?"

"I'm looking for Jimmy Nagel. Are you any relation?" I asked.

"No," she breathed, and hung up.

Okay. I tried B. A man's voice answered with a hearty, "Nagels!"

"Hi!" I sang back, just as heartily. "I'm looking for Jimmy Nagel—"

"Yeah? Who's this?" the man asked.

"A friend of a friend," I said.

"Ha! Well, okay. Who's your friend?"

I took a beat to answer. "Are you Jimmy Nagel?" I asked.

"I've been accused of worse. Who's your friend?"

"Connie Jones," I said.

"No shit? Man, that is bizarre," he said. "Connie fucking Jones. She told you to call me?"

"She mentioned your name, yes," I said.

"Damn, this is kinky. Twice in a week I hear the names of old buddies from high school. Guess that happens when you come back home," he said.

"The other buddy wouldn't be Trish Glancy, would it?" I asked.

"Whoa. Lady, you are spooky. That's exactly right!"

"Is there any way we could meet, Mr. Nagel? For lunch tomorrow, maybe?" I asked.

"You haven't told me who *you* are, babe. Don't you think that would be polite?"

I laughed. "You're right. I'm sorry. My name's E.J. Pugh, and I'm a friend of Connie's. I know this is weird, but I wondered if I could ask you some questions about Trish?"

"Hey, whatever floats your boat," he said. "But I don't go out. You'll have to come here. You can bring me lunch. A milk shake. Chocolate. From McDonald's."

"Okay. What time?"

"Anytime. The door's open. Just come in and holler. Bye."

* * *

The next morning, after I dropped the kids off at school, I went into Codderville to Vera's to baby-sit Garth while she went to her standing hair appointment. We played Chutes & Ladders, told stories, and tried to dress one of Vera's dogs up in doll clothes. That didn't go over well—with the dog anyway. Garth and I found it to be great fun.

We watched the first half of "Mr. Rogers' Neighborhood," then took a nap. Vera came home at that point, a little more silver and a little curlier than when she'd left.

"Gorgeous," I said.

"You are such a brat," she said.

"I mean it!"

"Well, I like it," she said, throwing her pocketbook down on the couch and storming into the kitchen.

I followed. "I like it, too!" I demanded.

"Don't suck up," she said, opening the refrigerator and glaring at the interior.

"I'm not!" I screeched.

"Hush, you'll wake the baby," she said, slamming the refrigerator door and staring at the pristinely clean sink. "Gotta clean this mess up," she said.

There was nothing in there. Not even a drop of water.

She leaned down and got the Ajax out from the cabinet and liberally dosed the sink with it. Then she grabbed her scrub brush.

"Vera, I like your hair. I think it looks lovely," I said. "I really, really do. You may choose to believe me or not!"

Vera turned and looked at me, a perplexed frown on her face. "What are you going on about now?"

I shook my head and left.

The address for B. Nagel in the phone book was in Codderville, not too far from Vera's. It was a small two-bedroom frame house, painted gray with white trim and red shutters. Two large pecan trees graced the front yard and old, heavily blossomed azalea bushes bordered the cement steps to the porch. It was a very pleasant little house.

I walked up the steps and rang the doorbell. When no one answered, I remembered what Jimmy had said on the phone. I tried the doorknob and it turned. I opened it and called out tentatively, "Jimmy? It's E.J. Pugh!"

"Hey, come on back. Just follow the sound of my voice."

The front room was sparsely furnished, and what furniture there was had been pushed up against the walls. That room opened into a dining room. The large oak table in there had also been pushed up against the wall.

"Take the left-hand door in the dining room, I'm in the back bedroom," the disembodied voice said.

I followed it down the hall.

It was a hospital room, complete with hospital bed, wheeled bed tray, IV stand, and heart monitor. A wheelchair in the corner appeared to be gathering dust. The man in the bed bore no resemblance whatsoever to the picture I'd seen of Jimmy Nagel in the Codderville High School "Roarbook."

The man in the bed was beyond emaciated—he practically wasn't even there. Wisps of hair clung to an almost bald pate, and scabs dotted his face and what little I could see of his sunken chest under the too-big pajama top.

He grinned at me, the teeth large in the skeletal face. "Only thing I got left is my voice," he said. "And a real hankering for McDonald's milk shakes."

Damn. I'd forgotten the milk shake.

"I'm sorry—I forgot. I'll go—"

He waved my words away with a bony hand. "Don't worry about it. Next time, okay?"

"Sure," I said, trying to smile.

"Well, sit down here where I can see you. My eyesight's not what it used to be." He laughed. "I know, I sound like I'm eighty, not twenty-four, huh? 'Course, I look like I'm a hundred, but I try not to look in a mirror." He pointed around the room. "You'll notice there are none in here. My mom's been real good about that. Keeps telling me I look just like Brad Pitt." He smiled again. "Then I see other people's faces, and I know I don't."

I smiled. "Oh there's a definite resemblance to Brad," I said. "Especially around the eyes."

"You're good, E.J. Pugh." He reached out his hand, and I took it in mine. "You afraid of me?" he asked.

"No," I said. "I think I can take you."

He laughed uproariously at this. "Bet you could! Hell, bet you could ten years ago." His smile vanished. "I have AIDS. Does that make you afraid?"

"No," I said. "I don't plan on seducing you."

He laughed again. "That's not bad, E.J. Pugh. Not bad." He struggled a little on the bed. "Hit that button to lift me up, will you? Mom usually sits me up so I can watch my soaps before she goes to work, but she was running late today."

" 'All My Children'?" I asked.

"Does a bear have hair? Erica is my woman! And that Dimitri's not half-bad."

I pushed the button on the bed that raised the head, and helped him with his pillow.

"Okay," he said. "I know you didn't come here to play nursemaid. You said you wanted to talk to me about Trish?"

"Yes," I said. "I have to be honest with you. I didn't know Trish. But the cops are looking at my sister-in-law as the most likely suspect in her murder. I don't think she did it."

He nodded his head slowly. "So you figure maybe you can finger me as her killer and get your sister-in-law off the hook?"

I laughed. "Well, I hadn't thought about that—"

He shook his head. "Won't wash. If it had happened a year ago, maybe. I was ambulatory a year ago."

"Have you seen Trish since you've been back in town?" I asked.

He shook his head. "No."

"I'm just looking for some background on Trish," I said. "Anything I can find."

"Well, look at her stepmother, the unholy Mona. She's your most likely suspect," he said.

"That's what I thought, but Connie said as long as she didn't have to deal with Trish, and as long as she was still in the will, she didn't care."

He nodded. "Sounds right. I can't see Mona going

out of her way to kill Trish. If her body had been found in Mona's bedroom, then maybe."

I didn't want to ask the next question on my agenda. I liked Jimmy Nagel.

"Did Trish do drugs?" I asked, not knowing an easier way to get into the topic.

Jimmy shook his head. "Naw. I tried to get her to get high with me a couple of times, but it just wasn't her thing. She didn't like to drink either." He sighed. "Trish was heavy into reality. Which made it even worse when the voices started."

"You knew about the voices?" I asked.

"Oh, yeah. She'd tell me about them. At first it really bugged her. Flipped her out. Thought she was going crazy. Of course, she *was* going crazy. But when they really got to her—when she really was crazy—then she thought it was okay. She thought it was normal."

"Trish went to California—to Stanford—to go to college, right?" I asked.

Jimmy nodded. "Yeah, that's right. She wanted to be an anthropologist."

"I understand you went to California, too."

He looked at me quizzically, then smiled. "As I understand it, Trish was back from California long before I went out there. Besides, I went to LA. Wanted to be a movie star."

I smiled back. "How did it go?"

"Ever see *Bloody Mama and the Seven Dwarves?*" he asked.

"Missed it," I said.

"I was the first corpse. Gave it my all. Could have gotten in the sequel—*Bloody Mama Meets Sleeping*

Beauty—'cept this crap started up,'' he said, waving abstractly at his body. ''Couldn't work too well after that.''

''When was the last time you saw Trish?'' I asked him.

''Trish?'' he said, momentarily confused. ''Was she in *Bloody Mama?*'' he asked.

''No—''

''I was the first corpse in *Bloody Mama and the Seven Dwarves.* You ever see it?''

''No, sorry, Jimmy, I missed it. Can I get you something to drink or eat before I leave?'' I asked.

''You leaving?''

''I'm afraid so. But I'll come back to visit you.''

''Will you bring me a McDonald's milk shake? Chocolate?''

''You bet,'' I said.

He closed his eyes. ''I loved McDonald's shakes,'' he said.

There was a woman standing in the kitchen when I came out of Jimmy's bedroom.

''Hello,'' I said. ''I was just visiting Jimmy—''

''Good,'' she said, opening the freezer door and peering inside. ''He needs visitors.'' She turned and held out her hand. ''Barbara Nagel,'' she said. ''Jimmy's mother.''

She was a tall, thin woman, almost reaching my height of five-eleven. Her dark hair was salted with gray and cut in a short but stylish bob. She was wearing low heels and a business-cut pantsuit. Jimmy's mother was a very attractive woman, in a no-nonsense kind of way.

"I'm E.J. Pugh," I said, shaking her hand. "I came to see Jimmy about a friend of his—"

"Trish," she said, nodding. "He told me last night that you'd called. Not that he can tell you anything about her," she said stiffening. "He hasn't seen that girl in years. Thank God she either didn't know he was back or didn't care."

"You weren't fond of Trish?" I asked, leaning against the counter, ready for a long talk.

Mrs. Nagel opened the refrigerator and fixed herself a glass of iced tea. "Would you like some?" she asked grudgingly.

I nodded.

"No, I wasn't all that crazy about Trish Glancy," she said, handing me a glass of iced tea. "Or any of that crowd Jimmy ran with in high school. He never would have—" She stopped herself and shook her head. After taking a long drink of her tea, she said, "Ancient history. Nothing could be worse than what's happened anyway. My boy is dying."

"All those new meds—" I started.

She laughed bitterly. "Jimmy's allergic to everything—including aspirin. It's hard enough finding a painkiller that will work for him, much less anything else."

"I'm so sorry," I said. "I just met him today, but I like him."

She smiled. "What's not to like? Everybody's always liked Jimmy. That's why everything seemed so easy for him. If not, maybe Trish and her crowd would have left him alone."

"He seemed fond of Trish—"

"That's the other half of Jimmy—everybody likes

him and he likes everybody. That's how she was able to get him into drugs in the first place."

She slammed her tea glass down on the counter and looked at me. "Then she went insane and someone murdered her and my son is dying of AIDS. Now it's time for you to leave."

I set the glass down, thanked her, and left.

Nine

I cried all the way home. I didn't even know Jimmy Nagel, had never met him before today, had never heard of him before yesterday, yet I couldn't stand the thought of the loss. So much loss. So many people—smart, gifted, normal, ordinary, loved, unloved, beautiful, homely—so many people dead and dying.

At that moment I'd give anything to do what Willis had suggested the other night—go back in time, to the mid-seventies, when the biggest problem was how to get Richard Nixon out of the White House. The war was finally over, and we were hip deep in Watergate; but when you look back on that now—after all the other assaults to the office of the presidency—it seems like just a trifle. Everyone thought the world was going to hell in a hand basket. They really didn't know how right they were. We were still relatively innocent then.

Now we have AIDS, homelessness, rampant child abuse, talk radio, daytime TV talk shows exploiting the stupid and vain, venereal diseases I couldn't even pronounce, and marriages splitting up because of computer chat rooms.

It all made Watergate look like a little domestic burglary.

I thought about Jimmy's mother, Barbara Nagel. Somehow her story and Jimmy's didn't jibe. According to Jimmy, Trish never did drugs. He said she was heavy into reality. Yet Mrs. Nagel seemed to think Trish had been the instigator of Jimmy's drug use. Was that just the usual mother's excuse of her son "running with a bad crowd"?

I shuddered to think how little mothers really know about their children—especially when they're teenagers. My mother knew next to nothing about what was going on in my head or on the streets. Just like I would know next to nothing when my kids hit driving age.

Barbara Nagel needed an excuse for her son's behavior, and running with a bad crowd seemed to be a good one, although to my knowledge, and from what I'd been told so far, Jimmy was the only drug user in that crowd. Or was Mrs. Nagel blowing the drug use out of proportion as a way of denying that her son was gay? If he'd gotten AIDS from drug use, he couldn't possibly be gay, too. Was that what she was thinking?

I was getting more depressed by the minute.

I turned on the radio to an oldies station and sang at the top of my lungs along with Crosby, Stills & Nash.

* * *

When I got home the phone was ringing. My first mistake was in picking it up.

"Hello?"

"E.J.! It's Juney!"

"Juney! My God! Where are you?"

"I've been arrested. Please help me, E.J. I didn't do it!"

Jim Bob Honeywell was not exactly pleased as punch to help me when I called him and told him about Juney.

"You know Vera's gonna skin me alive if I do anything to help that girl," he said.

"Jim Bob, Vera wanted me to find Juney. Call her, she'll tell you."

"Wanna bet on it?" he asked me.

"I'm serious, Jim Bob," I said.

He sighed. "I know you are, honey. Have you talked to Vera?"

"No," I said, "but I'll call her now to clear it, if you want me to."

Jim Bob cleared his throat. "Well, now, my dear, I am a grown man. I can do that myself."

I grinned. "Great. Then meet me at thc station?"

"As soon as can be," he said, and we rang off.

I arrived at the station ahead of Jim Bob Honeywell. Luna led me back to the cells to speak with Juney. She was in the same cell Vera and I had shared a little over a year ago. Ah, memories.

"Juney?" I said as I approached the bars.

She was sitting on the cot, her head in her hands. Her hair was dirty and stringy, her clothes torn and stained. When she looked up, her face was streaked with dirt and tears. On seeing me, she burst into sobs and flung herself at the bars.

"I didn't kill anybody!" she wailed, grabbing at my hands through the bars.

I took ahold of her hands and squeezed. "I know that, Juney. Just tell me what happened."

"I don't know! I don't know what happened! I found her dead and I ran and then they found me and they said I did it and they brought me here and they booked me and I didn't do it!"

I attempted to wipe at the tears on her streaked face. "Try to calm down, Juney. Take a few deep breaths."

I did a couple of deep breathing exercises with her, attempting to calm her down. Finally, it seemed to be working.

"I need you to try to answer my questions, Juney. But I need you to stay calm while you do that. Can you try that for me?"

She suppressed a sob and nodded.

"Okay, great," I said, giving her my best "mom" smile. "You're doing great. Did you know the woman they found?" I asked.

She shook her head. "Trish. That's all I know. She said her name was Trish. But then once she said her name was Moon Glow, too, but I think Trish is more likely."

"I agree," I said. "How long did you know her?"

"She saw me on the streets in La Grange like a couple of weeks ago I think, and she invited me to come stay at her place. Then I find her 'place' is just that little lean-to in the woods."

"Was there anybody else staying there?"

"Not that I saw."

"How did she get your hat?" I asked. "And the deposit slip I gave you?"

Juney moved away from the bars, her face turning red. She refused to look at me. She didn't answer the questions either.

"Juney?" I said. "You have to tell me the truth. You have to tell me everything that happened."

"Why? What are you going to do with it? You become a lawyer since the last time I saw you, E.J.?" she said, sarcasm dripping from her tongue.

"No, but I have one on his way. Meanwhile, everything you can tell me can help me sort this out."

"What are you now, the Sherlock Holmes of the burbs?"

"Okay, fine," I said. "See you around, Juney."

I headed for the locked door back into the station.

"Wait!" she cried. "E.J., I'm sorry. Really. Don't leave!"

I turned around and faced her. "Tell me what happened."

Juney sighed. "She had this old car and she drove me out to the woods. When she showed me her 'place' I thought, well great, this isn't much better than the street. But she started showing me around like it was this big mansion or something, and I started thinking maybe this lady wasn't quite all there, ya know?"

I nodded encouragement.

"Then she said I could stay there but it would cost me."

"She wanted you to pay?"

Juney turned a little pink. "I told her I didn't have any money. She said for me to dump out my back-pack. I said no, so she grabbed my hat and she goes, 'Okay, I'll take the hat.' And I go, 'Fine, take the hat.' That night I woke up and she was sitting beside me going through my backpack. I asked her what the hell she thought she was doing and she shoved Garth's picture in my face, and goes, 'Mine! Mine!' I tried to grab the picture back, but she started slap-ping me and acting crazy. So I just got up and started running."

"And left all your stuff there?"

Juney nodded miserably. "Two days later I started getting really mad. I wanted my stuff—especially my picture of Garth, ya know?"

I nodded my head.

"So I hitched a ride back out there and went traipsing through the woods—" She stopped talking and shuddered.

"What?" I asked.

"I found her. Her head was bashed in. The place was a mess. I just ran. Didn't even try to get my stuff. This wouldn't be happening to me if I'd gotten my stuff!"

"Ever hear of fingerprints?"

She just looked at me.

"Were you sure she was dead?" I asked.

Juney shrugged. "She sure looked dead. I didn't touch her, though, if that's what you mean. I got out of there and called the cops from a pay phone—you can do that even if you don't have a quarter—and told them where she was, but I didn't identify myself."

"Juney—" I started.

Jim Bob Honeywell picked that moment to make his appearance. Jim Bob is a very good attorney, wins most of his cases and has done so for the last fortysomething years. A lot of the credit goes to the fact that he is an excellent attorney and knows the law better than anyone in the state. But some of the credit has to go to the fact that one look at Jim Bob Honeywell and you couldn't possibly think he'd back a guilty person. If Jim Bob Honeywell said someone was innocent, by God you believed they were innocent.

Jim Bob, in his Harris tweed suit, bow tie, and cowboy boots, with his thick head of white hair, his ramrod-slim figure, and his quaint and gentlemanly speech, brought a smile to the face of every juror everywhere—and put terror into the hearts of most prosecutors.

If I was innocently accused of a crime—or guilty of one for that matter—I could think of no one I'd rather have on my team than Jim Bob Honeywell.

He smiled sadly at Juney. "Miz Trublood—"

"Harrell," Juney said. "I haven't changed it back. It's still Harrell."

Jim Bob bowed his head and smiled. "Miz Harrell, then, I apologize. I'm Jim Bob Honeywell. Miz Pugh here asked me to come talk to you. How are they treating you?"

Juney shrugged. "Okay I guess. Can I get out of here?"

"I've asked them to push forward the arraignment, my dear, and I believe they'll do that little favor for me. Have you eaten?"

Juney nodded. "They brought me some lunch a while ago."

Jim Bob smiled. "That's excellent. I'm so pleased. Do you have any other clothing, Miz Harrell?"

Juney shook her head. "No, sir. Everything I had was at the clearing in the woods. They got it all."

Jim Bob turned to me. "Miz Pugh, do you think you could find Miz Harrell something a little more appropriate for appearing before a judge?" he asked.

Thinking quickly, I said, "Sure, I'll be right back."

I headed out of the jail, jumped in the van, and made a beeline for Vera's house. Juney and Brenna were close to the same size. Jim Bob was right: there was no way she could appear before the judge in her dirty, torn clothing.

Vera was standing in the kitchen, arms akimbo, staring at the back door when I burst in. "Well?" she demanded.

"She says she didn't do it," I said.

"Humph," Vera said.

"She needs clean clothes to appear before the judge. I'm going to borrow some of Brenna's," I said.

Vera crossed her arms over her chest. "Whatever," she said.

She followed me into Brenna's room, where I went to the closet, borrowing a longish "church" dress, a pair of simple flats, and some clean underwear. Then I went into the bathroom where I "liberated" a bar of soap, some shampoo, deodorant, and a towel and washcloth. I shoved all this into Brenna's dry-cleaning bag that hung on a hook on the back of her closet door.

I turned and looked at my mother-in-law, still with arms crossed, staring at me from the doorway of Brenna's room.

She turned abruptly and walked into her bedroom. I started to take my haul toward the kitchen, when she stopped me.

"She'll need a hairbrush and some hot rollers," Vera said, handing same to me. "This brush is brand-new—tell her I never used it. And she can keep the hot rollers. You gave 'em to me for my birthday a couple a years ago. Never been used."

"Okay," I said, taking the offered loot. Impulsively I hugged her.

She pushed me away, her face turning pink. "Get," she said, then marched back in her bedroom and slammed the door.

Judge Mead was not in a good mood. Luckily he was taking it out on the assistant district attorney, a Baby Huey kind of guy, about twelve—okay, very young—with a high voice that broke occasionally like it was still trying desperately to change.

"We're seeking first-degree murder here, judge," the poor baby said.

"That's stupid," the judge said.

"Sir?" Baby Huey squeaked.

"First-degree means premeditation, numb nuts," the judge said. "Have you graduated law school yet? Actually, have you taken any courses yet?"

"Yes, sir," the ADA squeaked. "I mean, I passed the bar, sir."

"In the United States of America?" the judge asked.

"Yes, sir."

"Your honor," Jim Bob Honeywell said, standing slowly from his place next to Juney. "I'm afraid this boy doesn't even have circumstantial evidence against my client. I ask Your Honor to release this little girl on her own recognizance."

"But Your Honor!" squeaked Baby Huey, "She's homeless! She's just gonna run!"

The judge looked at Juney. "Jim Bob, the boy's got a point. The girl's got no address, no ties to the community—"

That's when I discovered I was standing. "Sir, Your Honor," I said. "I'm Juney Harrell's sister-in-law. I'll be happy to have her put in my charge, sir. I'll take her home with me."

The judge smiled and looked at Baby Huey. "Well, now, I guess that's settled."

"Bail, Your Honor!" Baby Huey all but yelled.

"What about it?"

"Sir, you gotta set bail!"

"How much you thinking, son?" the judge asked.

Furrowing his brow, the prosecutor said, "Under the circumstances, Your Honor, the state asks for $2 million."

The judge laughed. Baby Huey blushed. Jim Bob smiled sadly and shook his head.

"Your Honor," Jim Bob said, again rising, "this little girl's got no access to that kinda money. I'm afraid that's just ludicrous, Your Honor."

"I agree with you, Jim Bob. Let's make it $25,000." The judge looked at me. "Honey, you got that kinda money or you wanna call a bail bondsman?"

I grabbed the construction checkbook out of my purse and hurriedly wrote a check for twenty-five grand.

And I thought, *Lord, am I in trouble now, or what?*

Lizzie Borden had more support from her family than I was getting, that's for damn sure, and they didn't even know about the bail. I took Juney straight to Vera's, with Jim Bob Honeywell backing me up. Luckily, Brenna had gone to pick my kids up from school, and all were there, adding a buffering effect.

On seeing his mother, Garth screamed, "Mama!" and went flying into her arms. Juney hugged her son to her, tears streaming down her eyes. Over her head, where she squatted holding her son, Vera shot me daggers that were aimed straight at my evil eyes.

Brenna said, "That dress—"

I went up to her and whispered, "I borrowed it from your closet. And the shoes. And some underwear."

One eyebrow went up at the indignity of that. "She can keep 'em," Brenna said, no doubt under the negative influence of my mother-in-law.

Vera turned and fled the room, not having one word for either Jim Bob or myself. And certainly no word for Juney.

"Juney, are you hungry?" I asked.

"I could cat," shc said, still holding on to her son.

I headed for the kitchen, and Jim Bob headed for Vera's bedroom. I didn't envy him the experience.

I opened a can of soup to heat on the stove, and fixed some cheese and crackers on a plate. By the time Juney was sitting at the table, with Garth next to her, the back door opened and my husband walked in.

Willis looked at Juney, looked at me, and said, "Living room."

Jim Bob and Vera were not in the living room; my three kids and Brenna, however, were. "Brenna, take the kids to your room, please," Willis said.

Without a word, Brenna did as she was asked. Or told. Or whatever.

Willis stood in front of me, not exactly towering—he is six-foot-three, but I'm five-eleven, and he's not really *that* much taller. His arms were crossed, and he didn't look exactly pleasant.

"What the hell are you doing?" he asked.

"Willis, your mother asked me to find Juney—"

"Did she ask you to bring her into her home?" he demanded.

"What was I supposed to do with her?"

"You really don't want my suggestions, do you?"

"Honey—"

"Where's my mother?" he demanded.

"In the bedroom," I said. "With Jim Bob."

Willis turned on his heels and headed for his mother's bedroom. I was left alone in the living room—no doubt to contemplate my sins.

Jim Bob, Vera, and Willis came out of the bedroom about the same time Juney and Garth came out of the kitchen. Everybody stared at everybody else for a brief moment, then started busily looking at anything else they could find.

"Why don't we all sit down?" I suggested.

That's when everyone decided to look at me. None of the looks were friendly. But they all did sit down.

"Garth, why don't you go in Brenna's room? All the kids are in there," I said.

He grabbed his mother's neck. "I wanna stay with Mama," he said.

Juney kissed his cheek. "I'm not going anywhere, baby. You go play with your cousins for just a little while."

Garth hopped down and went down the hall to Brenna's room. Now it was just the adults.

No one said a word. Finally, I broke the silence. "Jim Bob, can you tell us where we stand?"

He nodded, obviously happy to be dealing with the business end of the situation. "They don't have very much evidence. They'll try to take this to a grand jury, but I'm not sure it'll wash. Our biggest problem could be appearances. Ms. Harrell, you need an address before this goes to the grand jury. You should not appear to be homeless."

I started to say "She can use ours—" at the same time Vera was saying, "She can use mine."

Jim Bob smiled. "We'll work that out to everyone's satisfaction. I will need to know where you've been since the body was found, why you ran. We'll need to convince the police—if not the grand jury—that you had no reason to kill that woman."

Juney nodded her head. "This is so bizarre. I just can't really take all this in."

"Well, you've had several days to think about it,

young lady,'' Vera said. ''It's not like it didn't occur to you that somebody might suspect you murdered that poor crazy woman.''

Juney stiffened. ''I never thought anybody would think I did it!''

''Then why did you run?'' Vera demanded.

''Because I thought the killer was still there! I was afraid!''

''Humph,'' Vera said, crossing her arms over her chest while Juney fumed beside me.

These two were definitely oil and water.

''Where have you been since you found the body?'' Jim Bob asked.

Juney shuddered. ''In Codderville. I tried the shelter, but it was full. I ended up staying in this vacant building with some runaway kids. I think they were all high on something. One night they tried to steal my shoes.'' A tear splashed from Juney's eye. ''My shoes were just about all I had. So I hit this girl—kicked her in the face—and ran. I stayed a couple of nights in a field in back of the Exxon station. Then I . . .'' Juney dropped her gaze. ''Then I stayed with someone for a few days.''

''Who?'' Jim Bob asked.

Juney shook her head. ''I don't know his name.''

My mother-in-law's body stiffened; I could almost see the ''tsk, tsk'' forming on her lips.

Luckily Willis spoke up for the first time since reentering the living room. ''I think it would be best if Juney came home with us,'' he said.

The kids picked that moment to troop in from the bedroom.

Mama!'' Garth cried. ''You're not going, are you?''

Juney turned to me, anguish in her eyes. ''Can't he come with us?'' she said.

Vera stood, her face a stone mask. ''I'll get his things,'' she said, then stiffly left the room.

Since we had both cars at Vera's, we split up, with me taking everyone in the van except Graham and Willis, who went in Willis's Karman Ghia.

I fed everybody, then sat the kids down in the living room with a video while Willis went to do his nightly inspection of the construction job. Juney and I sat at the breakfast-room table, she with a cup of coffee, me with a cup of tea.

''She really hates me, doesn't she?'' Juney asked.

I had no doubt she was talking about Vera. I shook my head. ''She's had a rough time, Juney,'' I said.

Juney laughed bitterly. ''Yeah, she's had it rough. One husband for fortysomething years, two kids who loved her. I know she lost one, but, E.J., the son she lost was my husband, you know?''

I choked back the ''of three weeks'' that immediately sprang to my lips, and just nodded. If I'd lost Willis three weeks into our marriage, it would have killed me.

''She hasn't seen Garth in so long, Juney,'' I started.

''If I ever felt welcome there, maybe I would have brought him by. But I know how much she hates me.'' She shook her head. ''Not a lot of incentive to drive a coupla hundred miles for a visit, huh?''

''Where were you living?'' I asked.

She took a sip of coffee. ''Houston,'' she said.

''What brought you back here?''

Juney looked out the sliding glass doors of the breakfast room to the darkened backyard beyond. ''It's home,'' she said. ''More or less.''

''Who'd you leave your other kid with?''

We both started at the deep voice behind us. Willis was standing in the kitchen doorway. The abrupt, nasty question was his.

''Willis—'' I started.

Juney stopped me. ''I suppose he has a right to know,'' she said. ''I'm staying in his house.''

''You don't have to tell him anything you don't want to,'' I said, ignoring my husband.

She turned in her seat to face Willis. ''Remember Bob? My husband? Bob Harrell. He's the one I was with when I came and got Garth last time.''

Willis nodded.

''We have a little girl I named Laurel. She's two and a half.'' Juney smiled. ''She's really cute. And funny. And smart as a whip. Just like her big brother.''

''Where is she?'' Willis demanded.

''Things didn't work out with Bob and me. He was seeing other women. So we got a divorce. He wanted custody of Laurel, but I fought him. Got me a lawyer and everything. But he wasn't a very good lawyer. Bob kept dragging me back into court, over and over. I had a job working at a dry cleaners, but I lost it because I missed so much work. Well, when the judge found out I didn't have a job, he gave full custody of Laurel to Bob.''

''But you got weekends and holidays, right?'' Willis

demanded. ‘‘Didn’t it seem like a good idea to stay in Houston so you could see your kid occasionally?’’

‘‘I got sick. Pneumonia. I didn’t have a job. Didn’t have any insurance. All my savings went to doctors and medicine and food for Garth. I couldn’t pay the rent. They evicted me after three months.’’

‘‘You had pneumonia for three months?’’ Willis said disbelievingly.

‘‘No, I had pneumonia for three weeks. But I was run-down, and I had a cough, and every time I’d go on an interview, and start coughing, the people couldn’t wait to get me out of their offices. I was supposed to be paying Bob child support, but I didn’t have a dime, so he wouldn’t let me see Laurel. And he wouldn’t help me. I even asked him for money once, and he just laughed at me. So Garth and I got kicked out of our apartment. I sold our stuff at a flea market and got enough for two bus tickets to Codderville.’’ Juney laughed. ‘‘I guess that was my—what?—tenth mistake? Sorry, I lose count.’’

‘‘So you come straight to Codderville and dump Garth on Mama and take off, huh?’’ Willis said, his voice rising.

‘‘No!’’ Juney said, her voice matching his. ‘‘I went to my mother’s house first! She wouldn’t even let me in the door! She’d never seen Garth in her life and she had no desire to see him then! Said I was nothing but trouble and to go away! That’s when I went to Miz Pugh’s!’’

‘‘Well, your mother was right about one thing—’’ Willis started.

I stood up, facing my husband. ‘‘Don’t say it,’’ I warned.

Willis snorted. "I don't believe a word of this shit!"

He turned and stormed out of the room.

Juney jumped up and headed for the back door. "I've gotta get out of here!" she said, grabbing at the door.

I grabbed her arm and pulled her away. "Where are you gonna go? You run away now, they'll lock you up so fast it'll make your head spin! And what were you gonna do? Just leave Garth again? Leave it to me to tell him where his mama's gone?"

"They hate me!" Juney screamed, her voice a loud whine. "Both of them! I never did a fucking thing to them, but they both hate me!"

I pulled her roughly over to the table. "Sit down!" I demanded.

She sat, face in hands, tears of misery splashing the table.

"Try for just one second to see someone else's side of things, Juney. Look at what Vera sees when she looks at you. She doesn't know you. All she knows are facts: You married her son, got in a fight with him and he died—"

"I didn't have anything to do—"

"Two: You're pregnant and you live with her and let her pay for everything—"

"She wanted to—"

"Three: You have the baby, then run off and leave him—"

"The doctor said it was postpartum—"

"Four: You come back a year later and take him away from her—"

"He's my son, for God's sake—"

"Five: You show up here four years later and leave him again—"

"What was I supposed to do? You don't know—"

"Juney, just shut up! Stop making excuses! Look at the facts! Just look at the facts that she sees. Not at your excuses and your reasons. Just the hard, cold, not-so-pretty facts! Vera is a woman who sees things in black and white. She doesn't know from gray, Juney. She knows right and she knows wrong—"

"It's not my fault she's an intolerant old bitch—"

I reached across the table and grabbed her arm. Tightly. "Stop," I said, my voice soft. "Don't say things that are just going to make it worse. I know you have your reasons. I know things aren't all black and white. But I also know if I were to talk to your ex-husband, I'd get a totally different story—"

"Well, he'd be lying!" she said.

"Or telling his own version of the truth, Juney. We all have our own versions of the truth. And Vera has hers. Her truth is the facts—without justification or explanation. Just the facts. And in her eyes, those facts damn you."

"What about my truth?" she said.

"What about it?" I asked.

She threw her arms up in the air. "Doesn't that mean anything to anyone?"

"It means something to you," I said. "So hold on to it. Know that it's your truth, whether others believe you or not. But just as you have your truth that you know is real, so does Vera. So does Willis."

"So what's the fucking point?" she demanded.

I shrugged. I had no idea what the fucking point was. That was my truth.

Ten

That Saturday at the Pugh house was about as much fun as root canal without the benefit of anesthesia. Willis stayed either in our bedroom or the backyard, surveying his domain. He didn't speak to Juney. Juney didn't speak to him.

The kids, picking up on the tension in the house, were even more horrendous than usual—demanding, whiny, hitting each other, and just being all-around brats.

When Brenna came by the house around noon, I thought for a moment I actually had a reprieve. No such luck.

"Can we talk?" she said, coming in the kitchen.

"Sure," I said, indicating the breakfast room table. "Want a Coke?"

"Diet?" she asked. The girl weighs ninety pounds.

"Drink the real thing," I said, grabbing a sugar-filled Coke from the fridge. "It's good for you."

She popped the top and took a small sip. "E.J., I've decided on the scholarship," she said.

I knew what was coming. I braced myself.

"I'm taking the one Northwestern offered," she said.

I nodded. Chicago, that toddling town. That far, faraway toddling town.

She reached a hand out, touching mine where it rested on the table. "Are you all right?" she asked.

I smiled. "No," I said. "That's too far."

"It's the best deal. Even with out-of-state tuition I'll be saving money. And I talked to the dean last night and she said she could get me a job on campus—maybe at one of the dorms—which would mean a reduction in my dorm rates. Even if I were to go to UT, E.J., I'd still have to live in a dorm. It's too far to commute. And the dorms at UT are much more expensive."

"We've got money for you—"

She patted my hand again. "I know, and I don't think I can begin to tell you how much I appreciate that. And I plan on paying back every penny—"

"Not on your life," I said.

She smiled. "I'll be home Thanksgiving. And Christmas. And spring break."

I shook my head. "You'll be home Thanksgiving. And maybe Christmas—unless you have a roommate who lives someplace really cool and invites you home. By spring break you won't remember where Codderville is. You'll be off to someplace tropical."

Brenna got up and walked around the table to hug me. "I love you," she said.

I hugged her back. "I know," I said. "I love you, too. I'm just finding it hard to let go."

She leaned back and smiled at me. "Better get used to it," she said. "You're gonna have to go through this three more times."

That's when I burst into tears.

We went to church Sunday morning as an extended family. Juney wasn't crazy about the idea, and Willis wasn't crazy about Juney coming along, but I was cheerfully adamant. I know, I was getting on everybody's nerves.

Liz Jones was seated two pews away during the service; afterward, I excused myself from my family and cornered her.

"How'd it go with Connie?" she asked.

"Great. She gave me a lead, and I followed that up. I don't know that it got me anywhere though."

She nodded toward Juney, who was walking out the door behind Willis, Garth holding her hand.

"Is that—" Liz started.

I nodded my head. "They arrested her, but Jim Bob Honeywell got her arraigned on bail, under my supervision."

"What does she say?" Liz asked.

"That she didn't do it." We both shrugged at that one. "Liz, I need to ask you another favor."

She grinned. "You want me to introduce you to Mona," she said.

"You're a mind reader."

"I'm just surprised you didn't ask for that when

you came by last week,'' she said. ''Connie said she told you she didn't think Mona would bother—''

''That's also what the other person I talked to said,'' I confirmed.

''Well, I'm not sure I agree with that, '' Liz said. ''Mona will do whatever is in Mona's best interest, and we have no way of knowing what might have been going on with Trish. She might have contacted Mona and said she wanted to come home. Believe me, knowing Mona, that would definitely be motive for murder.''

''So how do I meet her?'' I asked.

Liz grinned. ''Leonard made us join the country club because he thought it would look good on his résumé,'' she said, speaking of her husband, the OB/GYN. ''I've gone twice. But both times Mona was there. As I understand it from my sources, Mona is always there—from at least eleven in the morning until four in the afternoon.''

''She a golfer?'' I asked.

Liz shook her head. ''Nope. A drinker. And my sources say she has a thing for the tennis pro. Not that it is or is not reciprocated. I have no idea. But I understand she likes to sit on the patio with a Mai Tai and watch his cute little buns on the court.''

''So?''

''So come by my house around eleven-thirty tomorrow and I'll take you as my guest to the club for lunch.'' She grinned an evil grin.

''Liz, you are my kind of woman,'' I said.

''Honey, I'm everybody's kind of woman.''

I left her and went to the parking lot in search of my family.

* * *

I called Vera that night. She answered on the second ring, just as Brenna picked up the extension in her room.

"I need to speak with Vera," I said.

"I got it, honey," Vera said. Brenna hung up. "What?" she demanded, her voice nowhere near as nice to me as it had been with Brenna. Go figure.

"I need to go somewhere tomorrow around noon. I'm not sure how long it's going to take," I said. "I need you to baby-sit Juney and Garth."

There was dead air on the other end of the line. Finally she said, "You want me to come there?"

"I'll bring them to you if you want," I said, hoping she'd feel more at ease in her own home.

Again silence. Then, "Okay. What time?"

"Around eleven?"

"Fine," she said, and hung up in my ear.

Well, I told myself, *she's trying.*

Yeah, my other self said, *trying my patience.*

I stayed in the car. I waited until Vera opened the door to Juney's knock, then hightailed it out of there. I wanted to make sure Juney actually went into the house, but I also wanted as far away from that particular situation as I could get.

I drove back to Black Cat Ridge and to Liz Jones's house. It was a beautiful May day, the sun shining and the temperature in the high eighties. Liz was standing with her hip resting on the trunk of a bright red Miata. I pulled the van into her circular drive, giving the Miata room.

"Let's take my car," she yelled. "Glorious day for a ragtop!"

She was right about that. I didn't think about my carrot red hair clashing with the red of the Miata's paint job. I just let the wind blow my hair away from my face and grinned. God, I love a convertible.

We drove to the Black Cat Country Club. It's not like I hadn't been there before. I had. Terry Lester—Bessie's birth mother—and I had explored the country club thoroughly one Sunday—two weeks before it opened and sans escort. This was my first time back, but it didn't seem to have changed much since that first early exploration several years before.

It was a massive white rock, Mission-style building, with dark wood beams and lots of glass. It was surrounded by an eighteen-hole golf course—not the best in the state, but according to golfers I knew, not half-bad.

There were three clay and two grass tennis courts, an Olympic-size pool for adults only, and a kidney-shaped pool with waterfall and slides for families and children.

Inside were hardwood pegged floors, wool rugs, real wood paneling, crystal chandeliers, and suede love seats. There were also several meeting rooms equipped with computers, faxes, and photocopiers, two dining rooms—one seating a hundred, the other seating fifty, a grill, a bar, a ballroom, a racquetball court, and a full gym. Not to mention the reading room, the parlor, the dressing rooms, and the private dining rooms. The offices, kitchens, and laundry rooms were not meant for the gentry to see, and were hidden from sight and not nearly as well appointed.

(I knew this only from my clandestine tour with Terry Lester.)

The rock terraces also served as part of the dining room. You could order anything from the dining room, the grill, or the bar from the terrace. That's where Liz and I headed.

Several tables were already filled on this fine Monday. The one Liz headed to was occupied by a lone woman.

I'm not sure what I expected. If I'd had to guess what Mona Glancy looked like, I would have said "aging floozy." I would have been wrong. The woman sitting alone at the table we headed to was dressed in a full bathing suit covered by a matching skirt. The best way to describe her was as an aging Princess Grace. She was somewhere in her fifties, with champagne blond hair pulled back in a French twist, icy blue eyes, and skin that should not have been exposed to the sun as much as she obviously did. But basically she was a beautiful, classy-looking lady.

"Mona!" Liz cried, walking up to her and leaning down to hug the woman. "How are you doing?" she asked, her voice total solicitude. *Damn,* I thought, *she's good.*

"Liz, how delightful to see you," Mona said. Turning, she saw me. "And who's your friend?"

Liz grabbed my arm to her like the good buddies we were pretending to be. "This is my friend E.J. Pugh. Her husband owns Pugh Engineering Consulting in Codderville?"

It's one of those suburban things—a woman is most often introduced by what her husband does for a living.

"Oh, yes," Mona said, as if she'd actually heard of the two-man operation that is Pugh Engineering Consulting. "Nice to meet you," she said to me.

"It's nice to meet you. I'm so sorry to hear about your stepdaughter," I said, as Liz and I took unoffered seats at Mona's table.

"Dreadful," Mona said, shaking her head. "Poor Trish had so many strikes against her."

I could feel Liz tensing next to me. To head her off, I said, breathlessly, "Do they have any idea who did it?"

"Well, they've arrested some homeless woman," she said, leaning forward conspiratorially. "She must have bashed poor Trish's head in hoping to find money or something. God knows what those people think."

"Hope your husband doesn't plan any more layoffs," Liz said between clinched teeth.

Mona looked wide-eyed at Liz, unable, I suppose, to see the correlation between layoffs and homelessness. I thought about drawing a map, but figured it would be time-consuming and utterly useless.

"When was the last time you and your husband heard from Trish?" I asked, big-eyed in wonder and excitement over the nearness of something as exciting as murder. Well, at least trying for that. I could have looked like I was suffering from a hernia. I was kicked out of the drama club my junior year in high school for lack of aptitude.

"Months and months," Mona said. "My poor Edgar; he'd been trying to find her for so long. Hired private detectives and everything! And then we find out she was camping out just a few miles from us! It just broke his heart!''

"You hadn't heard from her at all?" Liz demanded, her tone not nearly as solicitous as it had been. "She never phoned?"

"Oh, goodness, no," Mona said. She laughed. "Poor Trish thought the phones were instruments of the devil. Or spacemen, or something. She had some fear of rays or some such rot zapping her through the phone wires."

The fact that she was laughing at her dead stepdaughter's mental illness was lost on neither Liz nor me. I stepped gently on Liz's toes, hoping to stop any retort.

"That must have been dreadful for you and your husband," I said. "Mental illness is such a strain on the family."

Mona rolled her eyes. "Tell me about it," she said. "That girl was looney tunes from the day I met her—and this was years before she was diagnosed, but I kept telling Edgar then that there was something strange about that girl—"

"I need a drink," Liz said, jumping up from the table. "Right now."

Liz stormed off toward the bar, Mona looking after her in wonderment. "Well, goodness, she could have waited. Enrique always waits on me. He'll be here in just a second—oh, here he is now! What was your name again, dear?" she asked me.

"E.J.," I said.

"Oh, right. What would you like to drink?"

I ordered a Coke and Mona touched her finger to

the rim of her glass and nodded slightly. Enrique took her glass, smiled, and hurried off.

"What was I saying?" Mona asked.

"That there was something strange about Trish—" I said, refreshing her memory.

"Oh, God, yes. First off, I mean, a lot of people lose their mothers at a tender age, but you would think that girl was the first it ever happened to," she said. Although she didn't add Vera's favorite editorial comment "tsk, tsk," I thought I could hear it somewhere in the lower regions of her mind. "She was inconsolable. Edgar didn't know what to do, and he asked me if I'd help. Well," she said, smiling sweetly, "what could I do? I said of course." She laughed bitterly. "You would think I was the Wicked Witch of the West the way she carried on. Telling me I couldn't go here and I couldn't go there—"

"Like where?" I asked, innocently quizzical.

Mona shrugged. "Her mother's bedroom for one. I was in her closet one day seeing if I could help Edgar do something about her clothes, and Trish came in. Well," she said, throwing her hands in the air, "you would have thought I desecrated the woman's grave! Trish just went crazy! She started screaming at me and pulling Madge's clothes out of my hands! I finally had to give her a Valium! My God, it was like she thought I would *wear* her mother's clothes!" She laughed and leaned toward me. "The woman was a good two sizes larger than me, not to mention she had absolutely atrocious taste! I wouldn't have been caught dead in her clothes!" She stopped, seemed to realize what she said, and covered her mouth while she giggled. "That was awful," she said. "Oops!"

Liz came back to the table, sans drink. Instead of sitting down, she just stood above me. "E.J., I have bad news. I just got a call on my cell phone. Leonard needs me to get home immediately, so—"

Mona looked up at Liz. "I thought you hated cell phones?" she said.

Liz smiled coldly. "I got over it," she said.

I stood up and held my hand out to Mona. "Great meeting you, Mona. So sorry about your husband's loss."

She shook my hand, then dropped it quickly as Enrique came back with her drink.

I left with Liz, sans my own drink.

Once back in Liz's Miata, I said, "We've got to figure out a way to pin this on Mona. Whether she did it or not."

Looking straight ahead, her usually friendly face bathed in a scowl, she said, "Let's just skip to the chase. And kill the bitch."

"That's an idea worthy of further thought," I said. I was kidding; I only hoped Liz was, too.

"Now you see why I have very little to do with my next-door neighbors?"

"Personally, I think I'd build a replica of the Berlin Wall between the houses."

"Poor Trish," Liz said. "That poor, poor child."

Eleven

I wanted to believe Mona Glancy did it. I wanted with all my heart to pin the murder on that cold-hearted bitch. But I really couldn't see her doing it. She could have chipped a nail.

I could see Mona hiring someone to kill her step-daughter, but I didn't think hired killers used blunt objects. In the movies they always had those neat cases with fancy take-apart guns. I never saw one of those guys open one of those expensive leather attachés and bring out a take-apart baseball bat. That just didn't happen.

Of course, all hired killers weren't like in the movies. Probably, the pros they show in the movies are the minority of hired killers. Willis told me once he met a guy in Houston who would kill someone for $50 and a Big Mac. Someone like that might use a blunt object. I mean, think about it: down on your luck, have to hock your gun, but you still need to keep working. It made sense to me.

How did I go about proving Mona Glancy hired a hit man?

I wondered if Willis still remembered the name of the guy who'd do it for fifty bucks and a Big Mac?

"What are you talking about?" Willis demanded later that night in bed.

"You remember!" I said, jabbing him in the chest with my index finger to help his thought processes. "You told me you met this guy who would—"

"Honey, I think I was exaggerating," my husband said.

"You mean he charges more?" I asked.

"I mean, if I remember the incident, I just sorta figured this guy was so low-rent he'd kill someone for very little."

I slapped his bare arm. "You lied?" I demanded.

He rubbed his arm and moved a little farther away from me. "That's not a lie. It was just a hypothesis."

I crossed my arms and sighed. "Great!" I said.

"What do you need a hit man for, honey?" he asked, leaning over and nibbling my ear.

"I didn't need a hit man—until I found out you lied to me!"

"It wasn't a lie," he said, pulling me down on top of him. "It was a slight exaggeration."

"But there are people like that, right?" I said. "People who will kill other people for very little and may not have those fancy attaché cases with the take-apart guns?"

Willis laughed. I hated it when he does that. I knew any minute now he was going to say the "C" word—as in "cute."

"Don't!" I warned him.

He sobered. "Yes, dear, there are people who will hire out to kill for what we would consider a small sum, and no they don't all carry fancy attaché cases with take-apart guns."

"Okay, great," I said, pulling away from him and sitting up. "Where would I find someone like that around here?"

Willis shook his head. "I don't know!" he said. "Why would I know something like that?"

"You were raised here!" I demanded.

"Like that means I know all the lowlifes in town, right?"

"Well, you gotta know some!" I said.

Willis started to retort, then got a pensive look on his face. Finally he said, "Jesse Maynard."

"What's a Jesse Maynard?" I asked.

Willis smiled. "The only real lowlife I ever knew. Great guy, too."

The next day Willis and I met for lunch at McDonald's and then went in his car to Sutter-Free. I had never been there. Back in the olden days, the Sutter-Free area of Codderville had been "colored town." Now, most of the town's African-Americans lived everywhere but there, and Sutter-Free had become the haven of bikers, crack-heads, and Codderville's one and only meth lab. Personally, I hadn't known about the meth lab until Willis pointed it out as we drove the narrow, winding lanes of the community.

Every clapboard house boasted at least one Harley; every tar-paper shack had a satellite dish.

I figured Willis had been right to bring the Ghia. My minivan would have stood out like a fart in church. Even so, we were watched closely as we drove deeper into the section.

The morning had started out hot and humid; now the temperature was dropping as clouds gathered in the east—big, black storm clouds. The wind began gusting, stirring up the dirt of the unpaved roads of Sutter-Free. I felt like we were in a Western movie.

Jesse Maynard's house was a small, one-story affair with old asbestos shingles trying desperately to look like brick. Mr. Magoo would not have been fooled. A pole from the street seemed to bring the place electricity, but the outhouse on the side made me worry about the plumbing.

Willis parked on the street, went to the driveway, and hollered at the house—not unlike, I supposed, visiting someone on a yacht. You hello the boat. We helloed the shack.

The door opened and a very skinny man, accompanied by an equally skinny dog, came to the porch. The man had bushy brown hair down to his shoulders, a full beard that had never been trimmed and seemed to reach from sightly below his watery blue eyes to his neck bone. He wore no shirt, exposing a hairless, concave chest. His blue jeans were stiff with dirt and the top button was undone, exposing an outie belly button. His age was basically indeterminate.

"Hey, Jess," Willis called.

The man scrunched his eyes against the sun, held

up a hand to shield his vision, and said, "Scooter, that you, boy?"

Willis grinned. "How you doing, man?" he said, walking into the yard. I followed tentatively behind him.

"Well, fuck me blind!" Jesse said, grabbing Willis's hand and pumping, then progressing into the man hug. Finally, Jesse pushed Willis away, his hands still on Willis's upper arms, and said, "Shit but if you don't look like a civilian!"

"One hundred percent," Willis said. He turned to me. "I'll prove it," he said. "This is my wife."

Jesse raised an eyebrow. "Legal?" he said, awe in his voice.

"Totally. Three kids, a mortgage, you name it."

"Aw, Scooter, man! Where'd you go wrong?" Jesse wailed. "It was UT, wasn't it? I told you going off to college would ruin you!"

Jesse gave me a look. "At least she's a looker," he said to my husband.

I was about to start kicking someone—at this point I didn't care who—when Willis said, "E.J. Pugh. Meet Jesse Maynard. Biggest, baddest motorcyclist in the whole damn world."

"And then some," Jesse said, taking my hand and pumping it. "Any woman can tame this boy is a whole lotta woman," he said.

I felt like I'd walked into a bad remake of *Easy Rider.*

"How do you do?" I said primly, much more primly than I would have in ordinary circumstanccs.

"Man," Jesse said, grabbing Willis again, "you need a longneck and a doobie. Ma'am," he said, nodding to me, "I'd be pleased to have you as my guest."

He ushered us up the porch step and into the shack. I knew how truly snobby I was when I recognized surprise at the cleanliness of Jesse's house. The floors were bare, unpolished wood, swept clean. The furniture was old, swaybacked and/or sprung, and the only stains were of the permanent variety; the bed I could see through an open doorway was only a mattress on the floor, but the covers were made, and the kitchen, a lean-to next to the room we were in, was clean. The only smells in the house were a light fog of tobacco and marijuana smoke.

Jesse went to an antique icebox in the kitchen lean-to and pulled out three Lone Star longnecks, and invited us to sit. I chose an old armchair that looked a little less sprung than the other furniture. Jesse handed me the beer.

"Now what are you doing here, man? Haven't seen you in, what, twenty years?" Jesse said.

"Must be," Willis.

Jesse looked at me. "Willis was a real good ol' boy till he went off to that no good university and got himself all tied up with them hippies," he said. He lit a joint the size of a cigar, and said, "Never did take to them hippy-types."

Willis grinned. "I wasn't a hippy, Jesse. Just a free spirit," he said.

Jesse said, "She-it," and passed Willis the doobie.

Willis waved it away. "Gave it up when I had kids, man. But thanks anyway."

"Ah, hell. I got kids. My oldest scores for me," Jesse said.

Exactly the point, I thought but didn't say.

"So what's up, Scooter?"

"You hear about that woman who got killed in the woods a couple of weeks ago?" Willis asked.

"The schizo piece got whacked? Sure, heard about it."

"My sister-in-law is the prime suspect."

"Well, fuck me blind." Jesse looked at me. "Your sister?" he asked.

Before I could answer, Willis said, "Dusty's wife."

Jesse shook his head. "Man, meant to, you know, come by, see you, whatever, when I heard about Dusty. Goddamn fucking shame is what it was."

Willis nodded.

"Didn't know he'd got hitched," Jesse said.

"Only married for three weeks, but long enough to leave a bun in the oven," Willis said.

"Fuckin' A, man. There's another little Dusty roaming Codderville?" Jesse said, a big smile on his face.

"Yeah," Willis said. "He's four years old."

"Damn, it been that long?"

"Almost five years since the accident," Willis said, his jaw set like it always is when he talks about the death of his baby brother.

Jesse leaned forward. "So what can I do for you, man?"

"My wife here, E.J., is looking into this. She's got a bit of a track record when it comes to finding out things."

"Yeah?" said Jesse, looking at me with what I wanted to believe was new respect.

"I've got kind of a wild theory," I said, smiling at Jesse.

"Ma'am, the wilder the better," Jesse said.

"Trish, the woman who was killed, has a real live evil stepmother. I'd love to pin this on her, but I can't see her doing it personally. So I'm trying to see if she could have hired someone to do it for her."

Jesse nodded and sucked smoke deep into his lungs. He held his breath for a second or two, then exhaled slowly. Personally, I thought I was beginning to get a contact high.

"So, basically, you come to me to see if I know anybody done a hit lately, huh?" Jesse asked.

"More to see if anyone around here is even in the market," Willis said, trying, I suppose, to be diplomatic.

"Oh, fuck, man, times are rough. We're still waiting for Reagan's trickle-down theory to work."

"That was two presidents ago," I said.

He grinned. "Exactly my point." His face sobered. "Now, you asking would somebody around here take a hit? Hell, yes. When you got kids and a jones to boot, you don't get real picky about what you'll do for the greenbacks, know what I mean?"

"Anybody been bragging?" Willis asked.

Jesse thought for a moment. "Well, not specifically, Scooter. Not about that schizo chick. But Tiny Malone came into some hard cash not too long ago, couple of weeks, maybe. Scored real big at the lab, even bought a couple of lids off my oldest. Saw him down at Fast Eddie's buying champagne cocktails for some pro."

"Pro?" I asked.

"Lady of the evening," Jesse said. " 'Scuse my French."

"We have hookers in Codderville?" I asked, my eyes probably wider and my voice a lot more naive than I would have wanted.

Jesse and Willis both smiled, and I knew we were getting really close to the "C" word. To head them off, I said, "So where do we find Tiny Malone?"

Jesse shook his head. "Ma'am, you and Scooter here don't want to go messing with Tiny. You know how some people get the nickname Tiny cause they're real big?" he asked.

I nodded my head.

"Tiny got the nickname cause his, excuse the expression, pecker is not what you'd write home to mom about. That kinda thing makes a man mean."

"I would suppose so," I said.

"But we try to tell him it's 'cause his head's so big," Jesse said, holding the roach of the joint with his fingernails and taking one last, long drag.

"So where can we find him?" I asked again.

Jesse shook his head. "Ma'am, you don't wanna find Tiny. I'll find him, ask around, get him loaded, see what I can find out. You got a telephone number?" he asked.

Willis took out one of his cards and wrote our home number on the back.

"Aw, Scooter, tell me it ain't so! You're a businessman?"

" 'Fraid so," Willis said.

Jesse shook his head as he walked us to the door. "And I had such high hopes for you, boy."

* * *

"Scooter?" I said, once we were back in the Ghia.

"A nickname is a sign of respect," my husband said, staring straight ahead of him.

"You belonged to a motorcycle gang?" I asked.

"Not really." He shrugged in a macholike fashion. "I rode with them some when I was in high school."

"*You* had a motorcycle?"

There was a beat before Willis said, "Not exactly."

"Excuse me?"

He sighed. "I rode one of Jesse's bikes," he said.

"Why didn't you get your own bike?" I asked, already knowing the answer.

Willis shrugged. "Never got around to it," he said.

I laughed out loud. "Never got around to asking Vera if you could have one, you mean," I said. "She'd have skinned you alive."

"You want to drop this?" Willis said.

"No," I said, still laughing.

"God, you've got a mean streak a mile long," my husband said.

I couldn't disagree with that.

Willis dropped me off at the McDonald's. The sky had darkened even more as we left Sutter-Free, and I looked to the north, to the building storm, as I got in the minivan.

I love a good storm. I always have. It energizes me—the drama of it, the excitement of it. Rain without lightning and thunder is just wet, but put the three together, and you have a night's entertainment a hell of a lot more stimulating than dinner and a movie. And sex during a storm is nothing to sneeze at—in case you weren't aware of this.

Since we'd moved to central Texas, there was a certain sadness for me about storms. In Houston, where I was born and raised and where I gave birth to my children, you can expect rain just about anytime. Droughts in Houston are such a rarity as to be laughable.

Not in central Texas. Each storm of spring could be the last one until fall; enjoy the one coming because you may forget what it's like before the next storm.

The air was cooling off and a breeze was picking up from the north. The smell of ozone was in the air, and the hairs on my arms were rigid with static. This one was going to be a gully washer—or, as my late father-in-law was fond of saying, "It was gonna rain like a cow pissing on a flat rock."

I drove over to Vera's, where I'd left Juney and Garth. When I got there, Vera's old Valiant was gone.

I got out anyway to check and see if the back door was open. I like to chastise my mother-in-law when I catch her doing that. The opportunity for this reversal in our roles is so rare I grab at the chance when it presents itself.

The wind whipped my hair in my face and tossed the newly green leaves on the sycamores in Vera's backyard. The back door was open and Vera and Garth were in the kitchen, both coloring in a book. I will admit Vera stayed in the lines better than Garth did.

"Hey," I said.

"Hey yourself," Vera said, then sniffed. "What is that smell?"

Oh great, I thought, *I reek of pot smoke.* Hopefully, that might be the one thing my mother-in-law can't identify with her bloodhound nose.

Vera stiffened. "Is that marijuana?" she asked.

I sighed and sat down. I should have known. "It wasn't me," I said. "It was a friend of Willis's." Ha! Put it on him, that'll teach him.

Vera smiled. "Haven't smelled that since I kicked Dusty out of the house that time," she said, and sighed with what looked like nostalgia.

"Where's your car?" I asked.

"Juney took it," she said, pronouncing her other daughter-in-law's name as she might that of the devil himself.

"Took it?" I screeched. "She's not here?"

"She had some errands to run," Vera said, not paying much attention to me.

"Vera! I could lose $25,000 if she runs!" I said.

"Shoulda thought about that before you got her out of the clink," Vera said, returning to her drawing.

"Mama will be right back," Garth said. "She was gonna get me some ice cream."

I smiled at the little boy. I wish I had as much faith in his mother as he did. "How long ago did she leave?" I asked Vera.

"Oh, about an hour ago," she said.

"An hour?" I screeched. "She could have gone to Brenham and bought the Blue Bell Factory in an hour!"

"Don't exaggerate," Vera said, picking vermilion out of the Crayola box.

"Where did she say she was going?" I asked, standing up and going to the window that looked out on the driveway, hoping to see the valiant old Valiant.

"To run some errands," Vera said succinctly, as if speaking to a slow-witted child. "She'll be back."

"Vera, you're not supposed to let her out of your sight!" I said.

Vera threw down the vermilion and looked at me. "No, Eloise. *You're* not supposed to let her out of *your* sight. I'm just doing you a favor!"

"Well, you're doing a piss-poor job of it!" I said.

That's when I heard the sputter of Vera's car in the driveway. I looked out the window and saw Juney getting out of the car, packages in hand, just as the sky opened up and poured rain.

"You may apologize to me now," Vera said, head held high.

"I'm sorry," I said, although we both knew I didn't mean it.

I opened the door for Juney and glared at her. "You're not supposed to go anyplace without me!" I said.

"Who says?" she said, slamming her packages on the table.

"The judge!" I yelled. "He released you to my custody!"

"Oh, really?" Juney said. "I was beginning to think he released me to Vera's custody."

Vera put her head down, but I still saw the smile

on her face. *Great,* I thought, *these two are going to finally get together, but it'll be at my expense!*

I took a deep breath. "I'm trying to find out who killed Trish," I said. "I can't do that and baby-sit you, too."

"I'm sorry, Nancy—I mean E.J. Forgive me."

Vera giggled out loud. Juney put a hand to her lips to hide the grin.

"Well, you two are something else," I said. "I'm so glad you're both having such a high old time. If you'll excuse me, I'm leaving now. Juney, you may come with me or stay here. Your choice."

Juney and Vera looked at each other and both rolled their eyes. And I felt a stab of jealousy. Go figure.

We drove back to my house with the windshield wipers on second speed. Lightning broke the sky and was followed immediately by bursts of thunder that rocked the van. The storm scared Garth, so we put him in the front seat, sharing the same seat belt as his mother.

"It's the clouds clapping," I told Garth, like I had told my own children at the same age. "Okay, every time you see the lightning, clap your hands real quick to beat the thunder, okay?"

The little boy looked at me dubiously, but tried it. After the third clap, he beat the thunder, and the game really began for him. The fear receded as the challenge took over.

I sneaked a glance at Juney, sitting there with her son, helping him catch the thunder. She certainly wasn't acting like a woman with a possible death sentence hanging over her head. I thought for a fleeting moment that maybe I should just forget this whole thing. Let her fend for herself. Yes, I can be downright petty at times.

When we pulled into the driveway, I saw that the entire structure was framed out. Which was the good news. There were no vans, no pickups, no nothing in the driveway. We were sans construction workers. This in itself was a good news/bad news deal: The good news was that I could exist in peace and relative quiet for a while; the bad news was that this just meant it was going to take that much longer to get the job done.

I went into the house and called Willis.

"The workmen aren't here," I said.

"I know," he said. "They called. It's raining. They'll be—"

"Raining?" I screeched. "Are they made of sugar?"

"E.J.—"

"When are they coming back?"

"Tomorrow or the day after—"

"That is not acceptable," I said.

"Honey, things need to dry out—"

"Can't we have someone doing something else while they're gone?"

"We're not at that stage yet," Willis said.

I hung up on him. Then, of course, I had to call back, apologize for hanging up, say goodbye, and hang up again. Life is not always fair.

Twelve

I was not happy. In fact, I was downright unhappy. I was living in a three-bedroom house with four children, three adults, a dog and three cats, and nary a workman in sight. And what did we even need them for? The whole idea had been to move Brenna in; now she was going off to Northwestern. And even if she were to come home occasionally, she'd still have Vera's room since Juney was back and she had Garth. Of course, this relied upon Juney's not winding up in prison for the rest of her natural life.

For a murder she didn't—or did—commit.

How did I know Juney didn't kill Trish Glancy? The woman stole all her stuff, was, by all accounts, nutty as a fruitcake. It could have been self-defense. Of course, if it had been, it might have been nice if the person she was defending herself against hadn't been the daughter of one of the leading businessmen in Codder County.

And it would have been nice if Juney hadn't run.

Hell, it would have been nice if she'd just stayed married to her philandering second husband so *none* of this would have happened.

Isn't it amazing how your morals can go so quickly by the wayside when it interferes with your life? Well, sometimes I find mine do, anyway. Personally, I believe a woman shouldn't put up with abuse—be it physical, mental, verbal, or psychological. And philandering is definitely psychological abuse.

On the other hand, what was a little screwing around when it could have saved me all this?

It was after nine before I got all the kids to bed. I thought to myself at least tomorrow there was school. For four more days. That was it. Then they were out and my life would become a living hell. I wasn't cut out for motherhood—I knew that, the kids knew that, and I think the PTA was taking up a petition for a declaration stating that very fact: E.J. Pugh is not cut out for motherhood. News at eleven.

I crawled into bed around ten, kissed my husband, read a chapter of a new mystery, and fell asleep with thc light on and the book on my chest.

At 2:00 A.M. the phone rang.

I reached over Willis's prone body and grabbed the phone.

"Hello?" I said.

"Hey, Miss E.J. This is Jesse. How you doin'?"

"Who?" I said.

"Jesse Maynard, Scooter's old buddy."

"Oh, right. Scooter." "Scooter" lay under me,

snoring away. I elbowed him in the ribs. He grunted, turned over, smacked his lips twice, and commenced to snoring. "What can I do for you, Jesse?" I asked.

"Ma'am, actually it's what I can do for you. Got Tiny right here in my house."

"Tiny?" I wasn't totally awake.

"Yeah, he's here, and he's more or less sedated," Jesse said and laughed. "Best time to talk to ol' Tiny is when he's toked up. He's a mean drunk, but he's a pussycat on smokin' dope."

"You want me to come over there *now?*" I asked.

"Is it too late?" Jesse asked, his voice curiously innocent. "It's just that Tiny likes his booze and he likes his speed, and both of 'em make him meaner than a junkyard dog. I thought now might be a good time, is all."

"Right," I said. "Ah, give me twenty minutes."

"Yes, ma'am. You take your time. And bring Scooter with you. Pretty woman like you shouldn't be wandering around the Free all by herself in the dark, know what I mean?"

"Right," I said, and hung up.

I elbowed Willis again. "Scooter," I said, "wake up."

"Um," he said.

I shook his shoulder. "Come on, big boy. Up and at 'em."

"Time zit?" he said.

"Almost seven," I lied. "We overslept."

"Shit!" Willis jumped out of bed and ran for the bathroom.

"No time for a shower, honey," I said.

He turned on his heels. "Right." He sniffed his

armpits. "I'll do." Then he looked at the bedside clock. He looked at me. "It's not seven. It's barely after 2:00 A.M.!"

"True," I said. "You missed a phone call from your buddy Jesse, Scooter me boy. We're due at his house in twenty minutes."

I got up and grabbed my blue jeans lying at the foot of the bed.

"You lied to me!" he said.

"A slight exaggeration," I said, and kissed him on the nose.

"Why do we have to go to Jesse's house?" he said, swaying a little where he stood.

"He has Tiny 'sedated.' Thinks this is a good time to interview him."

"It's 2:00 A.M."

"That's right," I agreed.

"We have children!"

"That's also true. But there is another adult in the house. I'll wake Juney."

"We're not supposed to leave Juney alone, right?" Willis demanded. "It was your bright idea to put *our* twenty-five grand up to guarantee her court appearance. And you're just going to leave her in the middle of thc night?'

"She'll be in charge of all the children," I said, pulling on a T-shirt. "She's too responsible to leave the children untended."

"Ha!" my husband said. Personally, I agreed with that assessment, but I had no other choice.

I guess I could have gone next door to Luna's house—Luna the cop—and said something like, "Excuse me, will you watch my kids while I go to the worst part of town to interview a stoned speed freak about a possible hit?" I don't think so.

I went downstairs to the sleeper sofa Juney was calling home, and shook her gently.

She was wide-awake before I even touched her. I guess that's something you have to learn living on the streets.

"What?" she said.

"Willis and I have to go out on an emergency. Will you watch the kids?" I asked.

She nodded her head. "What is it? It's not Vera?"

"No, nothing like that. It may be a lead on the Trish Glancy thing."

Juney looked at the LCD readout on the VCR. "At two-thirty in the morning?"

"Crime never sleeps," I said, and headed for the back door.

Sutter-Free was weird in the daylight. At almost three in the morning it was downright hellish, especially in the glistening wetness from the storm earlier. Where most places have that farmy, wet grass smell after a rain, the Free smelled strangely like wet dog.

We passed a few houses that were dark and quiet. Then we passed one lit up like a Christmas tree. There were a half dozen Harleys scattered around the front yard, some beat-up old vans, and a pickup or two.

"Somebody's having a party," Willis said.

This was further evidenced when the screen door of the shack burst open and a man came out backwards, flying off the porch and landing in the dirt of the yard. Another man flew out frontward, landing on top of the first man. A woman stood in the doorway laughing.

"And it's only Tuesday," I said.

We drove on to Jesse's place. A fifties Indian motorcycle was parked in the front yard, next to the Harley that had been there earlier. A light shone in the front room.

We got out of the Ghia and walked into the yard, my husband salivating at the sight of the Indian.

"Finest motorcycle ever built," he said, awe in his voice as his fingers lightly caressed the handlebars.

"Down, Scooter," I said. "Let's go."

With a sigh, Willis left the Indian, took the step up to the porch, and knocked lightly on the screen door.

The inside door opened, and Jesse grinned at us. "Took your own sweet time," he said. "I been wasting some of my best dope on this asshole."

He opened the door, and we followed him inside.

I cannot vouch for the size of Tiny's pecker, but he did have an unusually large head, the size intensified by the biggest Afro I'd seen since 1972. It was a frizzy blond mess which appeared to have been bleached and permed to the point of near death. He sat in the chair I'd occupied earlier, and cast bleary, red-streaked eyes at us. He grinned. Three prominent teeth were missing.

"She's cute," he said. "Hey, baby."

"Cool it, Tiny. She belongs to Scooter here," Jesse said.

Tiny looked at Willis. "Sorry, man. No offense."

"None taken," Willis said.

I, obviously, did not exist.

Willis, Jesse, and I took seats on the sofa opposite

Tiny. "Tiny here's been telling me about his recent brush with fortune," Jesse said. "Huh, Tiny?"

"Oh, yeah, man," he said, lifting his arm and taking a drag on the joint that had been resting near the floor. He breathed deeply and handed the doobie to me.

Even if I still smoked pot, anything that touched that mouth wouldn't touch mine. I handed the joint to Willis, who passed it on to Jesse.

"So?" I said to Tiny.

"Huh?" he said.

"Your fortune?"

"Oh, yeah. This old chick paid me some hard cash," he said, his eyes drooping.

"Who was she?" I asked.

"Some old broad," he said.

"What did she give you the money for?" Willis asked.

Tiny giggled. "Man, that's a secret!" He put his finger to his mouth and said, "Shhhhh."

Jesse said, "Ah, man, we won't tell nobody, huh, Scooter?"

"Shit no," Willis said. "Mum's the word."

"Who's Mum?" Tiny asked, his head beginning to loll on the back of the armchair.

"What did she pay you the money for, Tiny?" I asked.

"Cause I'm hot in bed, honey," he said. "Wanna see?"

"What did she look like, this old broad?" Willis asked.

"Like an old broad," Tiny said. "They all look alike."

"How much money did she give you?" I asked.

"A lot," Tiny said, his words beginning to slur.

"What did you do, Tiny?" Jesse asked.

"A little job," he said, his eyes closing.

"What little job?" I asked.

Tiny began to snore.

Jesse got up and shook him. "Hey, man, wake up! Don't conk out here!"

Tiny was dead to the world.

"Well," said Jesse, "y'all shoulda got here sooner."

"What's the chance that he'll tell you tomorrow?"

Jesse shrugged. "Slim to none."

I looked at my husband. "Some would definitely describe Mona as an 'old broad,' " I said.

He shook his head. "Honey, you're reaching."

I sighed. "Yeah, I know." I kicked Tiny in the shin. He smiled in his sleep. Willis and I thanked Jesse for his trouble and left.

It was very, very late (or very, very early actually, depending on how you see these things) when we got back to the house. All I wanted to do was fall into bed. Only there was one little problem.

Juney was not in the house.

"Fuck!" my husband said succinctly.

"Maybe she's upstairs," I said.

"Juney!" Willis hollered.

There was no answer.

I ran up the stairs and checked the bedrooms. The girls were sleeping soundly; in the boys' room, Garth snored gently. Graham raised his head, and asked, "What's up?"

"Have you seen Juney?" I asked.

He shook his head and let it fall back to his pillow, instantly asleep.

I went back downstairs where Willis was wearing a hole in the wall-to-wall. "What do we do now?" I asked.

He looked at me and laughed. It wasn't a pleasant laugh. "Well, now, dear, I don't really know. But since you're the idiot who got us into this mess, why don't you fix it for a change?"

I felt a need to do my Lady Macbeth imitation, but thrust my hands in my pockets instead. "Should we call the police?"

"What for?" Juney asked as she came in the sliding glass door.

"Where the hell have you been?" Willis demanded.

Juney turned a bright red. "In the backyard, sir," she said. "If that meets with your approval, sir!"

Willis glared at her, and she glared back. "Good thing the kids didn't need you while we were gone," he said.

"I was just outside!" she said. "I could have heard them!"

"Well, you sure as hell didn't hear us! And we've been screaming for you for—"

"Okay," I said, putting my bulk between them. "We're all tired. Let's just go to bed."

Willis glared at me, turned on his heels, and started for the stairs.

"E.J., I was just outside—" Juney began.

"Save it," I said, and headed in my husband's wake.

* * *

The next day was not pleasant. I'm not at my best on eight hours' sleep; four hours and I make Cruella De Ville look like Mother Teresa. I snapped at the kids, was rude to Juney, and refused even to speak to my husband—which was okay because he wasn't speaking to me either.

I did manage to get the kids to school and suggested Juney and I take Garth to my church's mother's day out. He was a sweet boy, and I didn't want to warp his mind by having him in my company for too long that day.

Neither Juney nor I spoke of the night before, but it was certainly on my mind. Where had she been? In the backyard like she said? If so, why? And if so, why hadn't she heard us when we pulled up, or when Willis was screaming her name at the top of his lungs?

And if she was lying? Where was she? I had to keep reminding myself that I didn't really know this woman. Who had I invited into my home? What could she have been doing at three or four in the morning?

I stole a glance at Juney as she sat in the passenger seat of the van, staring vacantly out the window. She was such a tiny little thing, seemingly lost in the great big world of being a grown-up. But that didn't stop the question: Where had she been?

One lone carpenter decided to come back to work that day, bringing with him what sounded like a chain saw, although I wasn't sure why we would need one.

I took a handful of Tylenol, went upstairs, turned

on the air-conditioning fan for white noise, and stuck two pillows over my head. After thirty minutes of the chain saw from hell, I decided I probably wasn't going to get any sleep.

Dinner sucked, and I managed to get the kids to bed by eight. I used as my excuse that tomorrow was the last day of school, and they'd need all their energy to party-hearty. Then I went upstairs, threw myself on the bed, and cried, thinking, *Only one more day before summer vacation.*

I felt physically better the next day, but was thinking about a nice, large prescription of Prozac to get me through the coming months, when the phone rang.

"Hello?"

"Is this the beautiful E.J. Pugh?" a male voice said.

I smiled, recognizing the easy baritone of Jimmy Nagel. "Every ounce of her," I said.

"This is Jimmy, remember me?"

"How could I forget our shared moments together?"

He chuckled. "Honey, you are good. Look, I got news, but it'll cost you a trip to my house and a McDonald's shake."

"Chocolate?"

"Does a bear have hair?"

He hung up, and I told Juney I'd be back later, grabbed the keys to the van, and headed to Codderville.

I bought two chocolate milk shakes at McDonald's and on my way back to Jimmy's bedroom I stuck one in the freezer for his mother to give him later.

He was sitting up in bed, looking no better—yet no worse—than the last time I'd seen him.

"Hey, cutie," I said, and leaned over and kissed his cheek.

"Flattery and kisses will get you nowhere," he said. "But if you brought me my shake, I'll tell you the location of the Seventh Fleet."

I handed him the shake and helped him fit the straw to his mouth. He took a long suck, then laid his head back on the pillows, a beatific smile on his face. "Ambrosia," he sighed.

"How you feeling?" I asked.

Jimmy shook his head. "We don't go there, honeychile. That subject is *verboten*."

"Okay. Why am I here, other than as a bringer of chocolate milk shakes?"

"There's no more noble an endeavor than that, my love. Seriously though, I wanted to tell you they're coming out of the woodwork. Cindy Belton called me."

"I don't know Cindy Belton," I said, hoping he wasn't having one of his less-than-coherent moments.

"Another chick from high school. You wouldn't know her," he said. "Anyway, she calls to make sure I heard about Trish, and I go oh yeah, I heard, what a shame, yadda yadda yadda, right?"

"Um-hum," I said encouragingly.

"Well, Cindy says Trish started calling her a while back. Really acting bizarre, wanting to come over. Cindy kept coming up with excuses not to see her, and Trish got worse and worse until Cindy had to change her phone number."

"That's basically what happened with Connie, too," I said.

"So does this help your case?" he asked.

I shrugged. "I haven't the faintest idea," I said.

"What was she doing?" Jimmy asked.

I shook my head. "I don't know. Maybe she had a copy of her yearbook and was just calling people at random," I suggested.

"Yeah, but if she was living in the woods, where did she get a phone?" Jimmy asked.

Then it hit me. "Shit," I said.

Jimmy tried to sit up. "What?"

I patted his hand, trying to get him to lie back down. "I just remembered something the evil step-mother told me," I said.

Jimmy rolled his eyes. "Darling Mona," he said. "What *did* the bitch say?"

"She said Trish never called her because she was afraid of the phone. That she thought it was the instrument of the devil or had evil rays from outer space coming through it or something. Of course, Darling Mona thought this was very funny."

"She would," Jimmy said. He stopped a beat, then his eyes got big. "But if she was calling Connie and she was calling Cindy—"

"Exactly," I said.

"She lied," Jimmy said, his skeletal smile showing wide on his gaunt face.

"Oh, yeah," I said.

"If you raise my arm, I'd love to try a high five," Jimmy said.

We managed it.

Thirteen

There was only one reason Mona Glancy would lie about Trish calling her. Because she killed her.

Okay, that didn't make perfect sense, but when you want something badly enough, you can fit almost any facts to any scenario.

Mona hired Tiny to kill Trish, then lied about Trish calling so that no one would know she had been in communication with her.

Made sense to me.

I drove the minivan back to Black Cat Ridge, but instead of going home, I drove to Sherwood Forest Village, home of my friend Liz Jones and her neighbor—the infamous Mona.

I started to pull into Liz's driveway, but another car was there. Not wanting to disturb her with company, I started to head home. That's when I noticed the baby car seat in the back of the new vehicle and the bumper sticker extolling the virtues of Codder County's Democratic state rep.

I figured the car belonged to Connie, and she was someone else I needed to talk to.

I pulled in behind Connie's car, and got out.

The two houses—the Joneses' and the Glancys'—were about a hundred yards apart, with foliage and trees and assorted landscaping separating the two. The Glancys' driveway was on the side of the house next to the Joneses'. There was a large oleander bush beginning to bloom separating the Glancys' driveway from the circle of the Joneses' driveway. Behind the oleander bush, I saw something.

A bright red, antique Indian motorcycle.

I knocked on Liz's door and simultaneously slipped inside, hissing "Liz!" as loud as I could without being overheard by the next-door neighbor. Who, of course, was behind closed and locked doors, probably with the air-conditioning on, and who was paying absolutely no attention to me. But there you go. Paranoia running rampant.

Liz and Connie came out of the back of the house, Connie with Ethan on her hip, slurping happily on his fist, which was stuck almost all the way in his mouth.

"E.J. . . ." Liz started.

"Shh!" I said, running to the living-room window that overlooked the driveway and the Glancy house next door. "Look!"

Everybody looked—including Ethan, who bent down from his perch on his mother's hip to see what the excitement was about.

"What?" Connie and Liz said, almost simultaneously, both looking out the window then back at me.

"That motorcycle!"

"Um-hum?" Liz said, giving me a look.

"I know who it belongs to," I said.

Liz and Connie exchanged looks.

"That's nice," Liz said.

"Who?" asked Connie.

"A biker who recently came into some money from what he called 'an old broad' for services rendered," I said.

"What services?" Connie asked, totally confused.

Liz and I exchanged a look. "Possibly for killing the old broad's stepdaughter?" Liz asked.

"GMTA," I said.

Liz raised an eyebrow.

"Great minds think alike, Mother, jeez," Connie said. "What are you two talking about?"

Liz was leaning down, looking out the window again, drawing the drapes back just far enough to expose one eye and part of her nose.

"How'd you find out about this?" Liz whispered.

"I have my sources," I said, getting on my knees to peer through the drapes below Liz.

There was a loud shrieking sound. I fell over onto the hardwood floors, and Liz jumped about a foot. Ethan laughed.

Connie took the two fingers she'd used for the piercing whistle out of her mouth. "Okay, somebody tell me what the hell is going on," she said. "Don't listen to Mommy," she told her son.

"A little swearing never hurt a child," Liz said,

taking her grandson from Connie. She collapsed onto the sofa, and said, "We'd better tell her everything."

I took an easy chair while Connie remained standing, arms crossed over her well-endowed chest, beautiful face scrunched into a frown.

"Tell me what?" she demanded.

"Your mother and I decided the most likely suspect for Trish's death is Mona. So we've sorta decided to prove it."

Connie rolled her eyes. "You two are out of your ever-loving minds! There's no way Mona would dirty her hands—"

"Precisely!" Liz said, beaming at her daughter. "That's why we decided she probably hired somebody—"

"Oh, for God's sake—" Connie started.

"And I managed to track down this biker named Tiny who came into some money from a quote old broad end quote—a lot of money, the way I understand it, and he won't tell what it was for—"

"So he's got a sugar mama, for heaven's sake," Connie said. "What has this got to do with Mona?"

I pointed out the window. "That's his motorcycle out there."

"How do you know it's the same motorcycle?" Connie asked, skepticism obvious.

"Because it's an antique Indian. They're very rare. There can't be more than one in this entire area!"

"So he's humping Mona!" Connie said.

I shuddered. "I doubt that seriously. You haven't seen Tiny. Besides, the nickname comes from—Well, let's just say Mona could probably do better."

Connie continued shaking her head. "You two.

My God. Can't you just stay out of this? Let poor Trish rest in peace—''

''That's fine for Trish,'' I said, standing up, ''but what about my sister-in-law Juney? She's going before a grand jury in less than a week. And she didn't do it, Connie.''

Connie sat down next to her mother and took the baby into her arms. ''I'm sorry, E.J. I forgot about your sister-in-law. Surely they don't think—''

''Jim Bob says the evidence is all circumstantial. He can't see them indicting. Still . . .''

''But what if Mona didn't do it?'' Connie said, a breath of reason Liz and I could have done without.

''She did it,'' Liz said. ''And even if she didn't, who cares?''

''Mother!''

''What?''

''Liz, what's say we pay a little visit next door?'' I suggested.

Liz stood up grinning. ''My pleasure,'' she said.

Connie sat Ethan down on the couch, where he grabbed a pillow and stuffed it in his mouth, then she stood up, glaring at us. ''No! This is just stupid—''

''Honey, I think it's time you left,'' Liz said, gathering up the diaper bag and various and sundry other tools of the mothering trade.

''You two are not going over there—''

Liz headed for the door, with me on her heels.

''Now just stop it!'' Connie said.

''Lock up when you leave,'' Liz said, as we headed out the door.

Connie was right behind us, the baby in her arms. ''This is the stupidest thing—''

"Just keep your mouth shut!" Liz admonished her daughter.

I glanced behind the oleander bush. The Indian was still there.

"I bet she's paying him off," I said, whispering.

"I thought you said he already came into some money?" Connie whispered back.

"Well, maybe that was only the first installment. He's back for more."

"Or maybe he's blackmailing her!" Liz said and giggled. "That would teach her!"

"Mother!"

We got to the Glancys' front door and Liz rang the doorbell, which played the first stanza of "Love Is a Many Splendored Thing."

"*She* added that when she moved in," Liz said. I had no need to ask who "she" was.

No one answered our ring. Liz pushed the button again. Finally, we heard footsteps approaching the door. The large slab of oak opened against the chain. A bleary eye peered out at us.

"What?"

"Mona, honey, how you doing? We were just so concerned about you we decided to come over and see how you are. You remember my friend, E.J.? And Connie of course. Have you met my newest grandson, Ethan?"

"I'm busy right now—" Mona started.

"Oh, honey, I know how you must be feeling. This has been a rough time for you, I know. Just let me in and I'll start a wonderful supper for Edgar so you won't have to! How's that?"

"Ah . . ."

"A woman in your situation needs her friends around her," Liz said, and beamed.

No one, not even Mona, could forestall a barrage of Liz Jones's helpfulness. She closed the door and unlatched the chain lock, and we trooped inside.

Louis XVI would have felt a little out of place in the opulence of the Glancy home. I hadn't seen so much gilt since the passing of Liberace. Everything that wasn't gilded was white—carpets, woodwork, marble tile, some furniture fabrics—the ones without the gold threads running through them in various designs. The only splashes of color came from the heavily gilt-framed paintings hanging on the brocade-covered walls. None of the furniture looked strong enough to hold Ethan, much less three healthy women such as Liz, Connie, and me.

Mona looked nervously at the baby Connie carried, no doubt worried about emissions. Connie, with a sparkle in her eye, sat Ethan down on the white carpet where he began crawling hither and yon, chewing on whatever was available, while Mona paled visibly.

"What can I do for you ladies?" Mona asked nervously.

"Why, absolutely nothing, dear," Liz said. "We're here to help you! Now, just shove me toward the kitchen—"

"Thank you, Liz, but Edgar and I are going to the club for dinner tonight."

"Well, how about if I make a few casseroles and just stick them in the fridge—"

"Carlotta hasn't done the grocery shopping yet this week, so there really isn't anything—"

"Well, I'll just go start making a list!" Liz said, grinning from ear to ear, and headed for the kitchen.

I went into the living room and sat down. There was nothing Mona could do but follow me. Connie leaned against the doorjamb into the living room, watching her son gum his way through the objets d'art.

"Who does that wonderful antique motorcycle outside belong to?" I asked Mona, my eyes big in wonder, my innocence a thing of beauty.

"My husband. He's just trying it out. I don't think he really wants to buy it," she said.

"Oh, really?" I said. "My husband knows someone who has one exactly like that! A guy named Tiny. Is he the one selling it?"

"I really wouldn't know," Mona said huffily. "Edgar would be the one dealing with that, not I."

"Well, tell Edgar to be careful! I understand this Tiny person is a bit, well, shall we say, unscrupulous?" I said, smiling sweetly.

Ethan had worked his way around the furniture and found Mona's foot, clad in the latest too-expensive, Italian footwear. Ethan stuck the tip of the shoe in his mouth, grabbed a handful of Mona's hosiery, and hauled himself to a standing position.

Either Mona's reflexes or her true nature caused her to kick out, sending Ethan sprawling. He landed on his rump and burst into one of those soundless cries. Connie and I reached him simultaneously just as the sucking in part of the cry was over and the blaring out part began. The young man had very good lungs, I must say.

Mona jumped up from the settee. "I'm so sorry," she said. "I didn't see him."

Right, I thought.

"This isn't the best atmosphere for a baby, is it?" Connie said.

Mona smiled sweetly. "We're not exactly baby-proof around here."

"I'll take him back to Mom's," Connie said, and hightailed it out the door.

Liz came into the foyer from the back of the house just as Connie left. "What's wrong with Ethan?" she asked, her hands deliciously dripping what looked like spaghetti sauce onto Mona's white marble floors.

"Mona kicked him," I said.

"It was an accident!" Mona said.

"Of course it was," I said soothingly, patting Mona on the arm. "I'm sure you're not really used to children."

Mona looked pointedly at the blood red ooze on the floor. Liz looked down and started—as if she had no idea what had happened. "I'm so sorry, Mona. I'll get something to clean—"

"No, no, that's quite all right," Mona said, herding Liz and me toward the front door. "You should go check on your grandson, don't you think? And thank you both so much for dropping by. Please come back anytime."

On the last word she shut the door in our faces. Liz and I stood staring at the large slab of oak. Then Liz looked at her hands, still covered with spaghetti sauce. Personally, I thought it was a little petty when she wiped her hands on the door, but then I guess even I'm above some things.

We walked back to Liz's house.

"How's Mona's kitchen?" I asked.

Liz grinned. "It used to be white."

When we passed the oleander bush, I noticed the Indian was no longer there.

I'd caught Mona in another lie. Edgar had not been home. Somehow the Indian motorcycle had been moved; ergo, someone else moved the motorcycle. Namely Afro-headed Tiny. He had obviously been in the house when we rang the ghastly doorbell; that's what had taken Mona so long to get to the door. And he must have walked the motorcycle to the end of the street because I'd been listening for the sound of the engine starting and had heard nothing.

Mona was looking guiltier and guiltier, I thought, smiling to myself as I headed for the kids' school. First she lied about Trish's use of the telephone; then she lied about the Indian. Both were definite lies. No way around that.

I worked up a likely scenario while I waited for the bell to ring signifying not only the end of the school day, but, alas, the end of the school year.

Trish had been calling Mona, threatening, more than likely, to move home. This would, of course, cramp Mona's style. The thought of living with her "crazy" stepdaughter pushed her to hiring Tiny to kill Trish. Maybe he was only supposed to scare her off, and things got out of hand. The end result, however, was the same: Trish was dead.

I thought about telling Elena Luna about this, then thought again. Luna and the other powers that be in Codderville law enforcement were quite happy with

Juney as a suspect. They weren't looking for anyone else. And Luna would not take me seriously without hard evidence; and hard evidence was something I didn't have.

I slumped down in the seat, depression stealing over me. All I had was what Luna would call a "wild theory," with nothing to back it up. What I needed was a confession from Tiny; barring that, maybe something concrete like a receipt for the blood money (do people actually give receipts for hits?), or a tape of the two of them in cahoots.

I wasn't able to get too far in my speculations because the bell sounded and all hell broke loose.

All the doors of the schools opened as if on timers, and kids of all colors, shapes, and sizes came bounding out, throwing notebooks and papers in the air, screaming at the tops of their lungs, and generally behaving as if they'd been let free from prison.

I saw Graham fly out the door with three of his buddies, all shaking their school papers out of their notebooks onto the cluttered school grounds. I felt sorry for the custodial services that day.

Megan came out another door with two little girls, all giggling, their heads together in conspiracy, each clutching a giant sucker. The sugar high in Black Cat Ridge that night would be awesome.

Finally I saw Bessie come out with her teacher, Mrs. Ackerman. They hugged and Bessie ran to the car, carrying a great big gold star; Bessie has a tendency to be teacher's pet, a position that has always pissed off her sister no end.

Bessie got to me first and I hugged her and congratulated her on the big gold star.

"It's because I had the highest grades and can read better than anybody else in my room, maybe even the whole school," Bessie said with a modest little shrug.

"Well, that's great, honey," I said. "You've always been a terrific reader."

"Can we go to the library on the way home?" she asked.

"May we go to the library," I corrected.

"Library? Yuck!" Graham said, jumping in the van. "I don't want to see another book for three whole months!"

"Forget that," I said. "We start Monday with the library summer-reading program."

Graham threw himself against the seat, letting out a groan that would have been appropriate for a sucking chest wound.

"What's with numb nuts?" Megan asked, working her way to the third seat of the minivan. One of the nice things about the minivan is that, unless Willis is in the car with us, none of the kids have to sit next to each other.

"Library!" Graham groaned, throwing himself across his seat and clutching his throat.

"Can we go now?" Bessie asked again.

"You have books at home that should hold you until Monday," I said, starting the van and moving into the slow flow of traffic. "Seat belts," I admonished.

Graham righted himself to grudgingly fasten his seat belt.

"Mine's already on because I'm not stupid like some people," Megan said from the rear.

"Good girl," I said.

"Mine's on, too," Bessie said from the seat next to me. "Mine's been on for a long time!"

"Well, what else would you expect from gold star Bessie?" Megan said from the backseat, her tone obviously derisive.

Bessie turned around in the seat, half out of her seat belt. "You're just jealous because you didn't get a gold star once the whole year and I got so many they gave me a special one today!" she said, holding up the huge award.

"Aren't you special?" my darling daughter said sarcastically.

"Some people think so," Bessie said dismissively, and turned her back on her sister.

"Ye gods," Graham said from the middle seat. "Three whole months of this?"

I could only silently agree.

Fourteen

I drove the kids with me to the new mall in Codderville. The next night was Brenna's graduation, and I still hadn't gotten her anything more than the gift certificate from the boutique. High-school graduation deserved something significant. I just didn't know what.

We wandered through store after store, with each child coming up with the perfect graduation gift: "Hey, Mom! This is cool! What about this?" from Graham, as he held up the newest in video-game equipment. "Mommy, she'd love this!" from Bessie, pointing at a foot massager, while Megan was busily trying to shove a huge stuffed gorilla into my arms as the absolutely best graduation gift in the world.

We ended up at Sears where I decided upon a not terribly original yet still significant gift: matched luggage. Brenna had come to us with an antique suitcase and two paper bags. No way would she be going off to Illinois like that. They weren't exactly leather—nylon actually—but two of the bags had wheels, and they all connected so you could pull a train of luggage across an airport terminal. I paid for the purchase—which the kids thought was boring and/or gross, depending on the child—and we headed back to Black Cat Ridge.

We got home to an empty driveway and the bare shell of construction. No workmen in sight. It had been three days and no sign of the crew, other than the one lonely carpenter the day before who appeared to have accomplished nothing more than aggravating my headache. There was still a hole in the wall from the utility-room to the outside, and only a padlock on the utility room door kept the world from the rest of the house.

There was still so much crap, however, in the backyard—nails, broken bits of wood, etc.—that there was no way the kids could go back there. Not to mention that my son, for sure, and probably my daughters as well, would use the half-constructed frame of the new addition as a jungle gym.

I got the kids in the house, poured them juice, then dialed Willis at work.

"Still no workmen," I said by way of greeting.

"I love you, too, honey," he said. "And I just love it when you call me in the middle of my busy day just for a little love talk. It's what keeps our marriage fresher than the rest."

"Are you going to call them, or what?"

"How was the last day of school?"

"You seem to be under the mistaken impression that we're having a conversation," I said. "We're not. I'm calling to complain because my house is a ramshackle mess, and it's all your fault. Now deal with it and don't give me any grief."

"You're beautiful when you're bitchy," Willis said.

"Goodbye," I said, and hung up.

Three small faces were looking up at me as I hung up the phone. They obviously expected something from me.

I walked into the living room in search of Juney. She was sitting on the sofa watching soaps, Garth on her lap.

"Let's get the hell out of here," I suggested.

Juney looked up, grabbed the remote control, and turned off the TV. I packed up kids, dog, and Juney, and we headed to Black Cat Ridge Park, on the banks of the Colorado, for a pre–Day One of Summer fun fest. At least there the kids could run and climb, as opposed to their own backyard.

Saturday morning was tryouts for soccer. The girls were now old enough for peewee soccer, and Graham was ready for his second year in "real" soccer. I drove to the fields with Juney and Garth as audience and watched the kids try out.

Graham, as aggressive as any X-chromosomer going, was picked in the first draft; Megan, who, like her brother, tends to take no prisoners, was also picked early. It was Bessie, the one of the more subtle genes, who didn't do as well. Because they don't want to leave any children out, she was picked for a girls' team consisting of three overweight girls and seven runts. Bessie, unfortunately, fit the runt category.

We all got back in the van with conflicting practice schedules in hand, and drove home. A huge Harley blocked the driveway.

''Wow, neat!'' Graham said, barely waiting for the van to stop before bailing out. He and his cousin Garth stood and stared at the giant motorcycle; I noticed Juney wasn't far behind.

''Wow is right,'' she said, staring at the Harley. ''Whose is this?''

''I wish I didn't know,'' I said, heading for the front door.

''Scooter'' and Jesse sat on the sofa, drinking longnecks and staring at NASCAR racing on ESPN.

''Hey,'' I said.

''Hey, your own sweet self,'' my husband said, lounging on the couch and lifting his face for a kiss.

I obliged while Jesse stood up. ''Ma'am,'' he said, tipping his head. ''Nice to see you again.''

''You, too, Jesse,'' I started, but then the front door opened and Juney and kids came bounding in.

Jesse didn't see the kids, or if he did, he totally ignored them. All he seemed to see was Juney.

The two stood staring at each other for a long moment before I figured out I needed to introduce them.

''Juney, this is Jesse Maynard, an old friend of Willis's. Jesse, this is Willis's sister-in-law, Juney Harrell.''

''Dusty's widow,'' Jesse said, holding out his hand to Juney.

Juney smiled sweetly at Jesse. "Is that your hog in the driveway?"

Jesse smiled back. "Yes, ma'am. Sure is. You ride?"

"Used to, but it's been a while."

"Maybe you'd like to go riding with me sometime?"

Oh, Lord, I thought. *Love's in bloom and I'm going to be sick.*

I turned back to Willis. "Any word from the carpenters?" I asked.

"No," he said, clicking off the TV, "and I'm beginning to get pissed."

"Beginning? I've been there and back again so many times I'm dizzy," I said.

"Carpenters?" Jesse asked, turning back to Willis.

"Yeah. We're doing some work on the house and this asshole I hired stopped after getting about half the beams up, and I haven't heard from him in days." Willis stood up. "Come on. I'll show you what I'm doing."

I'm doing, I thought. *Yeah, poor Willis, he's all alone in this.* Sometimes the only one who truly appreciates my sarcasm is me.

I got the girls upstairs to change clothes; Graham, however, was on his dad's heels, grilling Jesse about the Harley.

I went upstairs and shut myself in the bedroom; summer was officially here, and I needed to grab my privacy in little chunks while I still could. I was lying on the bed, my hand over my eyes, when I heard the door slowly opened. When I looked up, Bessie's head was peeking in.

"Mommy? You asleep?" she asked.

"No, honey," I said, sitting up. "Just resting my eyes. What's up?"

Bessie came into the room and hopped up on the bed. "I have a problem," she said, her beautiful little face serious.

"Whatever I can do to help I will, Bessie, you know that. What's the problem?"

Bessie sighed so heavily her body shook. She was silent for a moment, then said, "I really, really, really hate soccer."

"Oh?" I asked. "Do you really, really, really hate soccer, or do you just really hate the team you're on?"

"Both," she said matter-of-factly.

"You don't want to play soccer?" I asked.

"No," she said.

"I wish you'd told me this before I paid for the summer league," I said, trying to instill some fiscal responsibility—okay, bitching.

"You didn't ask," she said.

"What?"

"You didn't ask," Bessie repeated. "I think you just assumed because Graham loves soccer that Megan and I would, too. Well, you were right about Megan, but you were wrong about me."

"Well, okay, honey, if you don't want to play soccer, you don't have to," I said.

"I'd rather take gymnastics," she said, her face lighting up. "One of the girls in my class takes gymnastics right here in Black Cat Ridge at Mellison Dance Studio. They have all the equipment there and she's going to be in the Olympics. I want to be in the Olympics, too."

"Ah . . ." I started.

"I know I don't get an allowance right now," she said, "but I'm sure you're planning on giving me one someday. You can take the lessons out of that, okay? I just won't ever get an allowance, okay?"

Well, so much for her need to learn fiscal responsibility.

I hugged her. "Let me check into it, Bessie. I'll find out how much the classes are and if there are any openings for the summer, okay?"

She jumped down from the bed. "If there aren't any openings in gymnastics, I'll take ballet," she said. "Then I can go to New York and become a ballerina."

"Okay," I said as she scooted out of the room. It must be nice to have your whole life planned at seven—with options, I thought. Here I was with forty on the horizon and I still didn't know what I wanted to be when I grew up.

When I got back downstairs, Willis and Jesse were in the breakfast room, construction plans laid out in front of them.

"Ah, hell, this ain't nothing, Scooter," Jesse said. "Me and my boys can have this sucker up in a New York minute. And we'll only charge you what you haven't already paid that asshole who stiffed you."

I cleared my throat. Both men looked up. "Willis," I said, smiling sweetly, "may I speak to you in the living room, please?"

Jesse grinned at me. "Ain't gonna be that bad, ma'am. I promise."

Willis followed me into the living room. "What the hell are you doing?" I whispered angrily to my husband.

"Doing? Nothing! We're just talking."

"You are not going to give this job to a toked-out biker with no references!"

"Jesse has references!" Willis whispered back. "Hell, he built the town hall!"

"The town hall has been there since the early sixties!"

"Yeah? What's your point?"

I sighed. "What has he done lately?" I asked, enunciating succinctly, while still whispering. "Like in the last thirty-odd years?"

"God, E.J., you are really turning into a conservative housewife, you know that?"

I kicked him in the shin. "Take it back!" I said.

"Ouch," he said, moving away from me. "Straight Republican ticket next year, babe?"

I threw a couch pillow at him.

"Gonna have a Mary Kay party and start selling Amway?" he teased, keeping the couch between us.

"I will hurt you while you sleep," I said.

"Look at it this way," he said, coming over and putting his arms around me. "How much worse can Jesse's crew be than the last one?"

I wish he hadn't said that.

Graham refused to wear a tie. Megan couldn't find her Mary Janes. Bessie decided at the last minute she needed bangs and tried doing it herself, and Willis couldn't remember where he'd put his one and only set of cuff links. Juney didn't have a thing to wear—unfortunately literally—and Garth started throwing up for no known reason.

All in all, it was a miracle we were only fifteen minutes late getting to Vera's house to pick up her and Brenna for the first official Pugh family graduation dinner.

Brenna had chosen a Mexican restaurant on the banks of the Colorado. They had grudgingly allowed us to make reservations and seated us at a large table only ten minutes after we showed up. Considering the crowd at La Reyna that night, it was our second miracle.

We toasted Brenna with Shirley Temples and margaritas, ate nachos, fajitas, and flan for dessert, then headed to the Codderville High football field for the graduation ceremony.

We dropped Brenna off at the visitors' locker room—designated this night as the girls' dressing room—and went to find a parking place in the huge and totally filled parking lot.

Willis parked the car illegally in a red zone, and we all traipsed to the entrance, invitations in hand. Each graduate was allowed four invitations—Brenna had had to bargain with kids who only had a couple of people coming to get enough invitations for the entire Pugh clan. It's unfortunate how early young people understand the concept of scalping.

It was a perfect night. Because of daylight saving time, the sun had not yet gone completely down, but was making a lovely sunset to the west of the stadium. To the east, stars were beginning to appear in a cloudless sky.

The bleachers were full of parents and family—younger siblings running rampant up and down the rows. All four of our kids joined the fray, with a promise to keep an eye on Garth and to come back and sit with us once the ceremony began.

There were 312 graduates that night. Four arrangements for choir and chorus, two orchestra arrangements, four speeches by various school dignitaries, and a speech by the class valedictorian all had to be sat through before they began with "Aaron, Robert." Ninety minutes later they finally got to "McGraw, Brenna." We all stood up and cheered, hoping like hell to embarrass Brenna, but by the way she was beaming I somehow doubted we'd achieved our goal.

After another ninety minutes, they finally reached "Wyman, Judith." Then there was another short speech by the school superintendent and the throwing of hats and the screams of graduates.

I cried. You expected less?

We found Brenna in the crowd, she and Trent holding court with other friends, and congratulated them both. I took Brenna's cap and gown while the kids headed to the all-night party being thrown in the school gym. We could only hope they'd actually stay *there* all night—rather than the many alternatives eighteen-year-olds could think of.

I sniffled all the way to Vera's house, while she, my mother-in-law—my unemotional, stern, mother-in-law—blew her nose noisily in the backseat.

Our first child was leaving the nest—and we'd only had her for such a short while.

* * *

Jesse showed up with his "crew" bright and early Monday morning. The crew consisted of five guys on motorcycles and one driving a flatbed truck. One of the five on motorcycles was Tiny. This did not bode well for the new construction.

Keeping the padlock on the utility-room door firmly in place, I left Jesse and company to have their way with our backyard, and Juney and I took the kids to the pool.

One corner was the beginners' swimming class, and we enrolled Garth in that. My two had been swimming like Esther Williams since water baby classes, and Bessie wasn't too far behind them in this sport. Juney stayed with Garth while I sunned, swam, sunned some more, and swam some more. Swimming is one of the few exercises I like—you don't sweat when you swim; or if you do, you hardly notice it.

I was lying on a lounge chair turning my skin into a wasteland of freckles when I felt water dripping on me. I looked up into the tiny face of my nephew Garth. I sat up. "Hey, buddy," I said. "Your class over?"

"Uh-huh," he said, jumping on my lap. "Where's Mommy?" he asked.

I glanced around. "I thought she was with you," I said.

"Nope," he said, shaking more water on me and giggling.

I lifted him up and got off the lounge chair, perusing the pool for my sister-in-law. I spied my kids heading for the deep end—where they weren't supposed to go without an adult—and went over to head them off. "Have you seen Juney?" I asked them.

Three heads shook in a negative response, then headed underwater.

I went back to where I'd left Garth, and, taking him by the hand, started walking the perimeter of the pool, looking for Juney.

I was working with a lot of emotions, the number one being seriously pissed off. She'd done it to me again. Simply disappeared. Left her kid and disappeared.

With Garth in tow, I headed for the women's dressing room, just as Juney emerged.

"Where in the hell have you been?" I spit at her.

"I had to go to the bathroom," she said.

I handed her her kid and headed for the pool to round up mine. Maybe she had been in the bathroom, I told myself. Or maybe not.

We got back to the house at eleven-thirty, wet and starving. I parked in the street to avoid the motorcycles.

Juney took the kids in the front door, and I went around to the hole where the gate used to be to see how the construction was coming along.

Luckily I'm not the fainting type.

The beams had been torn down. In their place was a huge hole in the backyard, not unlike the beginnings of a very large in-ground pool.

"What are you doing?" I said—or screeched, or whatever.

"Ma'am," Jesse said, grinning at me and doffing his baseball cap. "Just getting started here."

"You're tearing it down!" I screamed. "You're supposed to be putting it up not tearing it down!"

Jesse nodded like what I said was perfectly reasonable—which it was, by the way.

"Yes, ma'am. I see where you're going. Problem is, the asshole—'scuse my French—who started this didn't do spit about a foundation. Gotta have a good foundation, ma'am, if you want the place to stand come time and winter, know what I mean?"

"We can't afford—"

Jesse smiled. "Now, ma'am, don't want you to worry your pretty head about any of that. Me and Scooter done discussed money, and, like I told him, I'm only taking what he already owed them assholes—'scuse my French."

"This is going to take forever!" I said, not one to be easily pacified by a dope-smoking biker wearing tie-dye.

"Well, now," Jesse said, spitting a disgusting wad of chewing tobacco in the general vicinity of my begonias, "we pour this afternoon, start the beams 'morrow morning, get up siding in the afternoon, gotta guy coming in for drywalling early Wednesday morning, should be ready for the plumbers come Thursday." He spit again. "That soon enough, ma'am?"

I just stared at him. Then turned and walked in the house. It's hard to argue with a dope-smoking biker wearing tie-dye, especially when he's right.

Juney kept coming up with reasons to go out in the backyard in her short shorts. I kept coming up with reasons to stare at Juney and Jesse through the still-standing glass doors of the breakfast room. Somehow a romance at this time between a semi-homeless woman soon to be under indictment and a biker who lived in a shack on the wrong side of town and scored dope from his son didn't seem wise. I'd go so far as to say it seemed almost foolhardy.

I spoke to Willis about it later that night in bed. "I think Jesse has designs on Juney," I said.

"Um," he said, his nose buried in the new Tom Clancy.

"And I think she wouldn't mind," I said.

"Uh-huh," he said.

"And I think the aliens who landed in the backyard just beamed up the children."

"Um," he said.

I grabbed the book and stuck it under my pillow, effectively losing his place.

"What?" he said, sighing that lovely Pugh sigh.

"I think a romantic attachment is brewing between Jesse and Juney, and I don't think it's a good idea."

Willis laughed. "Puleeze!" he said. "Jesse wouldn't—" He stopped and looked at the ceiling. "He's old enough to be her—" He stopped again and looked at me. "Shit," he said. "This isn't good."

"I think that's what I've been saying. What can we do to stop it? Can you talk to Jesse?"

"He wouldn't listen to me," Willis said.

"Does he know she's liable to be charged with murder any minute?" I asked.

Willis sighed. "That just might make her seem sexier to Jesse. In case you haven't noticed it, he's a little perverse."

"That's an understatement," I said.

Willis reached for the book stuck under my pillow. "Nothing we can do about it tonight," he said, searching for his place in the story.

"Like hell!" I said. "We can worry!"

"Um," Willis said, his nose firmly back with Tom Clancy.

As usual, in the worrying department, I was all alone.

By noon Wednesday, Megan was at soccer practice, Bessie was at gymnastics, Graham was visiting a friend, and I'd dropped Juney and Garth at Vera's. I was blessedly alone.

I was trying to conjure up some enthusiasm for turning on my computer when I heard a motorcycle start up. Looking out the breakfast-room window to the driveway beyond, I saw Tiny take off on his antique Indian.

I ran outside to where Jesse was watching the siding going up on the new rooms. "Where's Tiny going?" I asked.

Jesse looked at me, then at the driveway. "Oh," he said. "Something about a hot date. Should be back soon. Not to worry, we're way ahead of schedule."

I ran through the hole where the gate used to be to the street where the van was parked. I had a feeling I knew with whom Tiny's hot date might be.

I drove straight to Mona's house, parking at the end of the cul-de-sac, and walked purposefully toward Liz Jones's house next door.

Liz's Miata wasn't in the driveway. I walked up

her driveway, as close as I could get to the oleander bush.

The Indian was parked nose in to the bush.

I knew it! Liz and I had interrupted the payoff and Tiny had come back to collect. And I would catch at least the exchange of money. And if I could, maybe overhear something incriminating.

I worked my way around to the back of Mona's house, skirting the kidney-shaped pool, the expensive lawn furniture, and the lawn jockey whose face had been politically correctly painted a peachy beige.

I hugged the side of the house and worked my way to the nearest window. Crawling under the sill, I inched my way up until I could peek inside.

It was a nice room. It had a pool table. It was empty.

I stood up and inched my way along the rock facade of the Glancy house. The next window held an empty breakfast room. I was lucky it was empty. Even crawling on my belly I would have been exposed in the floor-to-ceiling bow window of the breakfast room. A higher window exposed an equally empty kitchen.

But out of the corner of my eye I could see movement in the next room.

I fell to my knees, hugging the wall. I'd found them. On my hands and knees I crawled slowly to the next window.

It was then I felt the hand grasp my Reebok.

Fifteen

I truly, finally understood the expression about the heart jumping to the throat. It went along almost simultaneously with a need to barf and an urge to pee.

I fell to my side in the wet mulch of the Glancy flower bed, instinctively striking out with my foot.

My three-pound Reebok hit my husband square in the nose. I managed to slam my hand over his mouth before the cursing got loud and out of hand.

"Shhhhh!" I whispered. "They'll hear you! What are you doing here?"

"Jesse called me. Said you went tearing off after Tiny. I knew exactly where you'd be going! Are you out of your mind?"

"I think that's a moot point. They're in that room," I said, pointing behind me.

"So what?" Willis demanded.

"So maybe we can see an exchange of cash or hear something!"

He grabbed my hand. "In case you don't know this, we're both trespassing! We're getting out of here!"

"Not now! I'm so close!" I jerked my hand away and resumed crawling toward the last window on this side of the house. I heard twigs snapping and branches breaking as my bull of a husband followed in my wake.

"Shhh!" I hissed behind me.

I was there. The window was an inch from my right eye. I hunkered down under the sill and slowly brought my head up.

It was a guest bedroom, done in Mona's usual ornate style. A large bed was enclosed in a gilt canopy with gauzy white material draped over it. The dresser and settee were French provincial in style, white with gold and gilt.

The one thing truly out of place in the room was all the black rubber. Some of Tiny's pale Afro escaped the rubber headgear he wore, but his ass was firmly defined by the black-rubber thong. Black-rubber tubing attached his arms to the end posts of the massive bed; more tubing kept his legs in a spread-eagle position.

I felt Willis crawl up next to me and heard his slight intake of breath at the sight before us.

Enter Mona, mistress of the naughty boys. I must admit for a woman of her age she had a very nice body.

The hip-length boots accentuated very shapely legs. Bare nipples poked out of holes in the black-rubber bra, and the crotchless black-rubber panties attested to the fact that Mona wasn't a natural blonde.

The black whip appeared to be made of leather, rather ruining the black-rubber motif as far as I was concerned.

"Have you been a bad boy?" I heard her say through the partially opened window.

"Yes, mistress," Tiny said. "I been real, real bad."

"Do you want Mommy to punish you?" Mona said.

Tiny wiggled his thong-defined butt. "Oh, yeah, Mommy, I need a spanking real bad."

I sat down on the ground, no longer able to watch the performance going on in the Glancy guest room.

"Let's leave," I suggested to my husband.

"Shhh," he said, "we're just getting to the good part."

I grabbed him by what little hair he had left and encouraged him to leave with me.

I followed Willis's Karmann Ghia back to the house. I wasn't happy. It was beginning to look as if my well-planned plot had holes you could drive Jesse's flatbed through. What if Tiny had been telling the truth? What if the money did come simply from being Mona's naughty little boy?

Or could it be both? Of course it could. It definitely could. Who else would one get to do one's dirty work but one's S&M consort? It made perfect sense. What I'd just witnessed didn't mean diddly; of course they were having sex—or whatever. Sex—or whatever—gives you a sense of trust with the partner, whether warranted or not. It made more sense than ever that Tiny and Mona had conspired to kill Trish.

Wouldn't she want Trish out of her life more than ever, given her penchant for bedroom antics with someone not Trish's dear old dad? With Trish living in the house, Mona might be forced to play her games at Tiny's abode—and I doubted seriously if Tiny had anything gilded.

Still, as I reached the house, I found myself somewhat depressed. I wasn't getting any closer to proving Mona responsible for Trish's death, and, truth be told, seeing Tiny's bare butt would be enough to send anyone into a slight depressive state.

Thursday I got a call from Jimmy Nagel.

"Hey, gorgeous," he said when I picked up the phone.

"Hey yourself, handsome, what's up?"

"Other than the fact that I'm in dire need of a Mickey-D's shake? Nothing much."

"I wish I could come by today, Jimmy, but I'm hip deep in mommy chores—school's out, in case you don't keep up."

"You have my deepest sympathies. How many rug rats do you possess?"

"Three of my own and a visiting four-year-old."

"Strange as it may sound, I wouldn't trade places with you."

"Can't say that I blame you," I said.

"Did you ever get ahold of Cindy Belton?" he asked.

"Who?" I grabbed a gallon jug of orange juice

out of Megan's hand as she started to pour it into a very tiny cup.

"The old classmate I told you about who was being harassed by Trish!" he said, obviously not pleased with my detecting skills.

"Oh," I said, "to tell you the truth I forgot all about it."

"Got something to write with? I'll give you her phone number and home address."

"Sure," I said, and copied down what he gave me.

"I think you should talk to her," Jimmy said. "She might give you a lead."

"At this point, Jimmy, I'm totally out of leads *and* enthusiasm," I said.

"Okay," he said. "You gonna be driving your little nephew to visit your sister-in-law in prison, or you gonna get somebody else to do that?"

"Jimmy, that's not fair."

"Honey, you're talking to a man who's twenty-four years old and looks like ninety. Don't talk to me about fair."

"Low blow."

"Ooo, don't say blow, it's what got me into this mess in the first place."

I laughed. "All right, all right. I'll go talk to Cindy."

"Take Connie with you. They used to be tight, and she'll at least get you in the door."

"Good idea," I said. "I'll be in Codderville later in the week to see my mother-in-law. I'll stop by with a couple of shakes."

"You're a good woman, E.J. Pugh. Bye."

Cindy's address was in Black Cat Ridge. I called

Connie at her home. She answered on a half ring; Ethan was obviously taking a nap.

''Hello?''

''Hey, Connie, it's E.J.,'' I said.

''Hi, E.J. What's up?''

I told her about my conversation with Jimmy and his insistence I interview Cindy Belton, and his suggestion I take Connie with me. ''When's the next time you plan on being at your mom's? I thought as long as you were here in Black Cat Ridge, we could go see Cindy together since she lives here, and Liz can watch Ethan.''

Connie sighed. ''E.J., I really don't want to get involved in all this—''

''Believe me, Connie, I understand. I have no intention of involving you. I just need you to introduce me to Cindy. We can take two cars if you want, and you can leave as soon as you get me in the door.''

''I saw Cindy last year at the five-year reunion. That was the first time since graduation, and we didn't have much to say to each other. She'll think it's pretty strange me stopping by like this.''

''Not after we tell her what's going on. And she's the one who called Jimmy. She's obviously willing to talk to old classmates about this mess with Trish.''

Again I heard Connie sigh. ''Okay, fine,'' she finally said. ''How about tomorrow? Mom and I are going shopping in the morning, then we were planning lunch at her house. I can put Ethan down for his nap after lunch and we can go over there. Okay?''

''Sounds great,'' I said. ''See you about one?''

''One o'clock's fine,'' Connie said, her voice resigned. ''Bye.''

I was back to having a plan; it made me happy. I didn't know what I could possibly learn from Cindy, or how it would help Juney's situation, but it was, by God, a plan. Sometimes you have to take what's offered and just smile.

The Glancy house was shut up tight when I passed it the next day, turning into Liz's driveway. I noticed there was no antique Indian motorcycle hidden in the oleander bush. Maybe this was Mona's day for ogling the tennis pro's butt, instead of whipping Tiny's.

I got out and rang Liz's doorbell. The door was opened by Ethan, who immediately lost his balance and fell on his butt.

"Hey, sweetie," I said, picking him up.

Liz was about two steps behind him.

"Our new doorman," she said, taking the baby out of my arms. He grabbed for a handful of hair and we spent a moment disentangling his sticky fingers from my do.

"Connie tell you what we're up to?" I asked Liz, as we walked back to the kitchen. The smell of something baking led me like an urchin following the Pied Piper.

"Yeah, wish I could go, but somebody's got to stay with the little dickens," she said, making googly noises at her grandson, to his infinite delight.

Connie was sitting at the kitchen table, a cigarette in hand.

"I didn't know you smoked," I said as I slid into a chair beside her.

"I quit when I found out I was pregnant with

Ethan,'' she said, taking a long satisfying drag. ''Started up last week.'' She shrugged and snuffed the butt out in an ashtray on the table. ''Disgusting habit,'' she said, waving her hand to dissipate the smoke.

I sniffed deeply. ''Yeah,'' I said, ''disgusting. I quit twelve years ago.'' I sighed. ''And I still want one every time I smell it.''

''Sorry,'' Connie said.

I breathed in some more. ''That's okay,'' I said wistfully.

Connie stood up. ''Well, I suppose we should get this over with. I called Cindy, and she's expecting us.''

''Great,'' I said. ''We can take my van, unless you want to go in separate cars like we talked about?''

Connie shook her head. ''In for a penny, in for a pound,'' she said. ''Besides, Mom wants me to stay so I can report back every word.'' She touched the back pocket of her jeans. ''I have a notepad so I can take notes.''

I laughed, and we headed out to the van.

Cindy Belton lived in one of the villages that started at about $150,000. The house was a copy of a New England saltbox, with a half acre of wooded front yard. The house was painted a deep red with dark blue shutters and trim. A Volvo wagon was in the driveway, amid a jumble of big wheels and tricycles.

I parked the van on the street, and Connie and I walked up to the shiny red door with the big brass knocker.

Cindy opened the door almost immediately. She

was a tall young woman, but still shorter, of course, than both Connie and me. She was thin except for what my husband describes as a "sticky-out butt," with mousy brown hair and big blue eyes. She had a good smile and a firm handshake.

She and Connie hugged, then we were led inside the house. There were small rooms decorated in the Arts-and-Crafts style that went well with the design of the house. The kitchen appeared to be the largest room on the ground floor and held a huge round table with four small children, ranging in age from seven to two, sitting around it with a large wad of Play-Doh.

Cindy introduced us to her children—Prudence, Seth, Adam, and Priscilla (yes, I too noticed a whole New England theme going on here)—and poured us tall glasses of iced tea. She checked the children's progress with their Play-Doh project, then directed Connie and me into the living room.

It was a pleasant room full of wood furniture, books, and children's pictures on the walls.

"God, it was just awful about Trish," Cindy said, getting to the heart of the matter.

"I know," Connie said, shaking her head. "Poor Trish."

"Well, you knew better than anybody that there was always something a little off with Trish," Cindy said.

"Jimmy Nagel said you called him about Trish," I said.

"Yeah. God, did you hear about Jimmy?" She shook her head and whispered. "AIDS. Course, he was always a little off, too." She laughed.

I pulled in my temper, reminding myself I wanted something from this woman, and asked, "You heard from Trish before she died?"

Cindy rolled her eyes. "God, yes! She called constantly! I ran into her at a grocery store in Codderville one day, and somehow she got my number and started calling. From the phone book, I guess, after I made the mistake of telling her my husband's name."

"What did she want?" I asked.

Cindy shrugged. "Who knew? She just kept saying I had too many children, like that was any of her business!"

"Too many children?" I repeated.

Cindy shook her head. "That's what she kept saying. 'You got too many, you got too many.' Over and over. Drove me nuts."

"How did you respond?" I asked.

"I just kept saying, 'No, I have exactly enough.'" Cindy sighed. "Didn't do any good no matter what I said. She just screamed at me—'You got too many!'—then I'd tell her I had to go, and I'd hang up. This went on every day for over a week until I talked my husband into having the number changed."

"It took you over a week to change your number?" Connie asked incredulously.

Defensively Cindy said, "My husband's in real estate. We simply cannot have an unlisted number. It was bad enough having to change it! As usual, Trish made a fine mess of my life."

"How's that, Cindy?" I asked.

She sighed and gave me a look. "Weren't you listening?"

"I meant, you sounded like she'd done this before."

Cindy tossed her mousy brown hair. "Trish was always jealous of me. Went all the way back to junior high, huh, Connie?"

Connie shrugged. "I wouldn't know," she said.

"Yes, you would!" Cindy accused. "Remember in the eighth grade, at Rita Muncy's house? The slumber party?" Cindy looked at me, anger playing across her face. "I fell asleep, and Trish put onion dip in my sleeping bag! God, what a mess! My mother was furious!"

Connie shrugged again. "Must have forgotten about that," she said.

"And what about that time at the senior prom? Surely you remember that! Trish shoved a needle into my lipstick and I scratched myself in the girl's room when I went to put on more lipstick! Actually started bleeding right there at the prom!"

"You don't know that was Trish!" Connie said.

Cindy made a "humph" sound. "Who else could it have been? She always hated me."

"Maybe it had something to do with your telling Michael Barnes that Trish had herpes right after he asked her out our sophomore year."

Cindy laughed. "Just getting back at her for the onion dip!"

"So," I said, trying to get back to more recent history, "that's all you can remember Trish saying when she called?"

"That's all she said! That I could understand anyways. God, she was a real mess! When I saw her at the grocery store, I swear she weighed less than eighty pounds and most of that was clothes! Dirty, nasty clothes.'' Cindy shuddered at the memory and made a face as if she smelled something bad. ''She always was pretty pathetic.''

Connie jumped up. ''No, Cindy, she wasn't,'' Connie said. ''She was shy and a little awkward and her mother died when she was way too young. And then she was stricken with schizophrenia. But even with that, she had a hell of a lot more class than you've ever had.''

With that Connie slammed out the front door. I looked at Cindy. ''Well,'' I said. ''if you think of anything else—''

''Just get out,'' my hostess said. ''Right now!''

I got out.

Once back in the car, Connie said, ''Sorry. I thought telling her off was better than beating her over the head with her antique spinning wheel.''

''You were entitled. She was getting a little out of hand.''

Connie laughed. ''The funny thing is, Trish didn't put the onion dip in the sleeping bag. That was me and another girl. And she also didn't put the needle in the lipstick. I'm pretty sure that was Jimmy.''

''Jimmy? That seems like a mean thing to do,'' I said, imagining the man I knew.

''You've only seen Jimmy the way he is now. In high school, he was a real prankster, and a lot of his jokes weren't very nice. I think he was probably sexually repressed, or whatever. But Cindy used to rag on him something fierce. She even sent a Valentine's card to this boy Jimmy liked and signed Jimmy's name to it. I think the lipstick was retribution for that."

"Then why didn't you tell Cindy that?" I asked, wondering why she would lay the blame for things she and others did on her friend.

"Trish loved it that Cindy thought it was her. She never had the gumption to do anything to Cindy herself, but she loved that Cindy thought she did."

"What do you make of what she said when she called Cindy? That 'You have too many kids' stuff?"

Connie shrugged. "Who knows? Maybe she could remember she didn't like Cindy, and was taking a shot."

We got to Liz's house and both got out. Ethan was still asleep, and Liz was on the phone. I took a proffered banana-nut muffin and said my goodbyes. It was time to round up the kids.

That night in bed I told Willis about Cindy Belton.

"Seems like our Miss Trish certainly knew how to make friends and influence people," he said.

"Cindy's a bitch," I said.

Willis raised an eyebrow. "And you've known the woman how long?"

"Long enough for her to make disparaging remarks about gays, laugh about AIDS, put down a woman for mental illness, and whine like a three-year-old about how unjustly *she's* been treated."

Willis nodded his head. "Sounds like a bitch," he said.

"I think I mentioned that," I said.

"But did you learn anything?" he asked.

I gave him a look. "No," I said.

"So where are we?" he asked.

I gave him another look. "Exactly where I've been all along. Mona, conspiring with Tiny, killed Trish to keep her away from the house."

Willis shook his head. "Sounds lame to me."

"Jump up my butt," I said.

"Don't try to distract me with sex," he said.

I hit him on the arm. "That was derisive, not sexual," I explained.

"Sorry, must have been thinking of Mona and Tiny."

"What a fun couple," I said, snuggling up to my husband.

The next day Juney and I took the kids to Vera's for lunch. I dropped them off early and headed to McDonald's for chocolate shakes, then drove to Jimmy's house.

The door was unlocked as usual and I put one shake in the freezer and took the other into the bedroom, calling Jimmy's name as I did.

There was no response.

Jimmy was in bed, his eyes closed. "Jimmy?" I said softly.

He opened his eyes and looked at me. "Yes?" he said.

"Hey, hope I didn't wake you," I said.

"Are you the nurse?" he asked.

"Jimmy, it's E.J. I brought you a Mickey-D's shake." I moved the straw toward him. He took a sip.

"That's good," he said, taking a small swallow.

"You okay?" I asked, knowing I wasn't supposed to.

"Yes, ma'am," he said. "I'm fine. Is Terrance here?"

I looked at the picture on the dressing table. He had told me once about Terrance, Jimmy's longtime lover who had died three years before.

"Not right now, Jimmy," I said. "But he'll come in when he gets back."

"Okay," he said, and reached with his mouth toward the straw. I moved it where he could reach it, and he took another swallow. "This is good," he said. "What is it?"

"A chocolate milk shake," I said.

Jimmy giggled. "Don't tell Terrance. He never lets me have sweets—says I'll get fat!"

"I won't tell," I said, holding the straw for another sip.

Jimmy's head went back on the pillow. "I'm sleepy," he said. "Tell Terrance I'll see him when I wake up."

"Sure," I said.

Jimmy closed his eyes, and his breathing became regular. I turned to leave the bedroom and saw Barbara Nagel standing in the doorway, resting one slim hip against the doorjamb.

"Why do you keep interrogating him?" she asked.

"I'm not," I said. "I just brought him a milk shake."

"He asks about that friend of his a lot. Terrance?"

I nodded my head.

"They were roommates," she said. "A lot of people think because he has AIDS that Jimmy's a homosexual. But that's not true. It was the drugs. Isn't it bad enough that I had a drug addict for a son? Do people have to call him a homo, too?"

I moved toward her. "Why don't we go in the living room?" I suggested. "You don't want Jimmy to wake up and hear you."

"Why not? He knows he's a drug addict. He knows he's not queer."

I gently took her arm and tried to steer her out of Jimmy's room.

"I don't like you," she said, pulling her arm from my grasp. "You're like that horrible Trish Glancy. I told her a thousand times I wouldn't let her talk to Jimmy—"

She stopped.

"When?" I asked. "You said she never called after Jimmy got back to town."

Barbara Nagel turned her back on me. "I meant before," she said. "Before Jimmy left town."

"No, Barbara, I don't think so," I said. "I think Trish called after Jimmy got back. Didn't she?"

Mrs. Nagel headed for the front of the house, her low, sensible heels clicking rapidly on the pinewood floor. She held the front door open. "I want you to leave," she said. "Jimmy doesn't need anyone but me. I take care of my son. Don't come back."

I stepped over the threshold but turned back to Mrs. Nagel. "Jimmy's my friend," I said. "And I'll come back whenever I choose."

"You'll come back to a locked door," she said, and slammed said door in my face.

I drove back to Vera's, seething. Who did that woman think she was? What right did she have to keep me away from Jimmy? To keep Jimmy away from people?

And just what did she have to do with Trish Glancy? Were phone calls the only contact Trish had tried to make with her old friend, or had she gone to the house? And been intercepted by Barbara Nagel? How far would Barbara Nagel have gone to keep Trish away from her son?

Don't be an idiot, I told myself, and tried to put it out of my mind.

I pulled into Vera's driveway, trying not to think about Jimmy Nagel and his Nazi mom. Brenna was working at the mall making extra money for college, but didn't start until one o'clock that day, so we all sat down to one of Vera's heavy-cholesterol dinners. Vera firmly believes that if God had meant for vegetables to be fresh, He wouldn't have invented the can opener.

"So how's the job?" I asked Brenna.

"Great," she said. She was working at the same boutique where I had gotten her the graduation gift certificate. "With my employee discount, I can get even more with that gift certificate."

"You bought anything yet?" I asked.

"Not yet. But there is this unbelievable suede jacket I have my eye on. Perfect for fall in the Midwest."

"I don't want to talk about it," I said, bending down to my plate.

I could feel eyes exchanging looks over my head.

"Wanna borrow my pinking shears for those apron strings, E.J.?" Vera asked.

"Don't you start," I said. "You're worse than I am."

"I'm learning," Vera said, applying herself heartily to the pot roast.

"When do you leave?" Juney asked. I wanted to kick her under the table, but I couldn't find her leg.

"Middle of August," Brenna said. "I need to get there a little early; first for freshman orientation and also because I'm going to be working in the office of the dorm and I need to be there before the kids start arriving."

"Is it a coed dorm?" Juney asked.

Brenna and I looked at each other. We'd been trying to keep that knowledge away from Vera, but I figured she'd need to know sometime.

Brenna nodded her head. "Yes."

"Coed?" Vera asked. "You mean like boys and girls in the same dormitory?"

"Yes, ma'am," Brenna said, bending over her plate and not looking Vera in the eye.

"Like right in the next room?"

"No," Brenna said. "Different wings. It won't be like I'll be sharing a bathroom with a boy or something, Miss Vera. Thank God." She stuck her tongue out at Graham and Garth. "Boys, as we all know, are stinky!"

"Ha!" Graham said, and his cousin echoed, "Ha!"

"As everyone is aware," my son said, "girls are gross and disgusting."

"Oh really?" I asked. I looked around the table. "Seems to me there are six females here and only two of you boy-types. You wanna say that again?"

"It would take six just to gang up on one guy because we're stronger and tougher," my son said.

I grabbed him and held him while Brenna ran around the table and gave him a noogie on the top of the head. "I'm next," his grandmother called calmly from her place at the table.

"Then me!" "No, me!" the girls argued.

Juney was laughing, Vera was smiling, Garth was giggling, along with my girls, and everyone was having a grand old time when the doorbell rang.

Always a portent of doom.

Sixteen

Brenna, being up, ran to get the door. She came back into the kitchen, followed by Jim Bob Honeywell.

Jim Bob smiled a sad smile and nodded at everyone. ''Hello, all,'' he said, then smiled at Vera. ''Vera, dear, how are you?''

Vera blushed. ''Just fine, Jim Bob.'' She got up from the table. ''Let me fix you some pot roast,'' she said, heading for the stove.

''Just a small portion, my dear. I've already had lunch, but a man would be a fool to pass up Vera Pugh's pot roast.''

''And your mama didn't raise no fools,'' Vera said, smiling fondly at Jim Bob.

Juney and I punched each other under the table and tried to suppress giggles.

Vera put a plate of steaming pot roast and vegetables in front of Jim Bob, and we all got back to eating. After several bites, Jim Bob wiped his mouth on his napkin and sat back. "As wonderful as usual, Vera."

"Thank you," she said, turning a pretty pink.

"I'm afraid I've come with some bad but expected news," he said, looking at Juney.

All the adults stopped eating, and some of the littler faces looked up to see what was going on.

"Graham," Juney said, "would you mind taking Garth into the living room to play?"

"Mama, I'm still eating!" Garth said.

"You can finish it later, honey," she said.

Graham got up, and I said, "Girls, go with your brother, okay?"

Bessie and Megan looked from me to Jim Bob to Vera; then they looked at each other and sighed. "They never tell us nothing!" Megan said, pushing away from the table.

"Anything," Bessie corrected as she followed her sister into the living room.

"Don't correct me! You don't know if that's right or not!" Megan said.

"I do, too—"

Vera, Juney, Brenna, and I turned back to Jim Bob.

"What?" Juney said, clasping her hands in her lap and sitting up straight.

"The grand jury meets tomorrow and the DA is taking the case to them. He wants an indictment against you."

"What are my chances?" Juney asked.

"I'm not going to mollycoddle you, Mrs. Harrell.

It is true they only have very circumstantial evidence against you, but they have none against anyone else. The fact that Ms. Glancy was the daughter of a very prominent citizen in this community means they'll want a quick indictment. I'm sorry, but I'm afraid our chances of a no bill are not very good. In fact, I think I might go so far as to say they're downright unlikely."

Juney's whole body wilted as he spoke.

I said, "I think there *is* evidence against another party."

Jim Bob raised an eyebrow and said, "Oh? And who might that be?"

"Mona Glancy," I said.

Jim Bob nodded his head sagely. "The wife of the most prominent man in the community. Stepmother of the deceased. You want to convince a grand jury full of people who are more Mrs. Glancy's peers than Mrs. Harrell's that a queen bee of Codderville society is mixed up in the murder of her own stepdaughter? As opposed to a—and please excuse me, Mrs. Harrell, I'm just saying what the grand jury will see—as opposed to an indigent, homeless woman."

I succinctly laid out all that I had learned about Mona and Tiny. Vera shot me a look and turned blood red when I described the scene in the Glancy guest room. Brenna giggled, and Vera suggested she leave the table.

"Not on your life," she said. "I can vote now, remember, Miss Vera?"

"Voting and hearing smut are two different things, young lady," Vera said severely.

"The smut part's over," I told Vera. "Actually,

my whole story's over. So what do you think, Jim Bob?''

Jim Bob Honeywell looked at me sadly. ''My dear, in this country we call America we need a little something called evidence. It might seem silly to some people, but it's been working for a while now, and as my daddy used to say, 'If it ain't broke, don't fix it.' ''

''But she lied!'' I said.

''No laws against that—federal, state, or local.''

''She said Trish didn't use the phone because of her illness, but that was definitely a lie! She called everybody and their brother before she died! And the only reason Mona would lie about it was because she was hiding something! And that something had to be that Trish had been in telephone contact with her—which believe me Edgar Glancy never heard about, I can guaran-damn-tee you that! And another thing—''

Jim Bob rested his hand on my arm. ''Eloise, dear, you're becoming overly excited. Please calm down.''

I took a deep breath. ''I am not overly excited,'' I said.

''Of course not, dear,'' Jim Bob said. ''Now, as for your, excuse the expression, evidence, I'm afraid that really isn't anything we can take to court. It will be your word against Mrs. Glancy's. You can say until you're blue in the face that she said this or that, and all she has to do is deny it.''

''Jim Bob, this is stupid! We all know Juney didn't do it! Mona Glancy and that Tiny person probably did it! Hell, even Barbara Nagel has a better motive than Juney!''

Jim Bob patted my hand and smiled at Juney. "I'm not going to even ask who this Nagel woman is. Of course we all know Mrs. Harrell did not commit this heinous act. And I will prove that in a court of law. However, I'm afraid, ladies, that we will have to go through the formality of a lengthy, time-consuming, and emotionally and financially draining courtroom ordeal. My fees, of course, are pro bono, but there will be other costs associated with a criminal trial of this magnitude—"

"We'll take care of it," I said, just as Vera said, "I got some CDs need cashing in—"

Juney stood up. "I don't know what to say to you people," she said, tears in her eyes. "You've been better to me than I deserve—"

"Juney, don't—" I started.

She held up her hand. "No, E.J., listen." She sighed. "Seems like from the moment I walked into your lives I've caused you nothing but grief, and it's not getting any better. Sometimes I just wish I could confess to this and put an end to it, but I can't say I did something I didn't do. Mr. Honeywell, I appreciate your services, I really do. But I would like for you to run me a tab. I know you're an expensive lawyer, and your time is valuable. And as for the rest of it, Vera, E.J., any money y'all spend, please keep a record. I'm gonna pay you back one hundred percent if it kills me." She sighed again. "And if I'm convicted and they send me away, I would like Vera to raise Garth. Mr. Honeywell, could you write me up something to that effect?"

"*If* the time comes, my dear. Not when." He smiled at her. "I'm a very good attorney, Mrs. Harrell. If I were a betting man, I'd put my money on an acquittal without a qualm in the world.''

Juney smiled back at him. ''I'm sure that's true, Mr. Honeywell. I know Vera and E.J. and Willis think you're the best, and I'd take their recommendation over anybody's.'' She suppressed a sob. ''Now if y'all will excuse me, I think I'm gonna go lie down for a minute.''

Vera stood up. ''Use my room, honey,'' she said, ''there's a throw on the foot of the bed.''

As Juney passed her, Vera reached out and took her in her arms and hugged her briskly. Juney looked at me, and I shrugged. There's always a first time.

Jim Bob took his leave and Vera put Garth down for a nap in Brenna's room. Brenna went to work, and the girls headed outside to play with the dogs while Graham popped a video game into Vera's VCR.

''I'll go check on Juney,'' I told Vera who was in the kitchen scrubbing up for the third time.

I headed to Vera's room and softly knocked on the door. When there was no answer, I opened it quietly and peeked in. The bed covers were wrinkled, but empty. Juney wasn't there. The bathroom door was wide-open. She wasn't there. I check Brenna's room, where Garth was napping, to see if Juney had decided to lie down with her son. That room too was empty of my sister-in-law.

I tried to push the panic down. If she was going to run away, I thought, now would be the time to do it—before the indictment. Of course, there went my $25,000. I went into the living room and out the front door. All the cars were accounted for in the driveway. But that, of course, didn't mean anything. Juney had made it quite a ways on foot before.

Then I saw her—on the corner of Vera's street, leaning against a lamppost. I walked rapidly toward her without her seeing me.

"What the hell are you doing?" I asked.

She jumped, then threw the cigarette she was holding on the ground behind her. "Nothing," she said, turning red.

"Smoking?" I said, incredulously.

"No, I just . . . I mean, I don't—"

"Is that what this has been about? You sneaking off all the time? You're sneaking smokes?" I screeched.

Juney sighed and wrapped her arms around herself. "I'm a grown woman, and I can smoke if I want—"

I started laughing. I couldn't stop myself. "My God," I said. "I was thinking all sorts of terrible things about you! And you're smoking!"

"I promised Garth I'd stop, but things have been so stressful lately—"

I hugged her. "Juney, if you get Garth's permission, you can smoke anywhere you want to. Including my living room. Just don't sneak off anymore."

Brenna called in sick to work and stayed home with the kids; the rest of us trooped down to the courthouse to show a united front for Juney. We waited out in the hall with Jim Bob Honeywell when it was Juney's turn to go inside the grand jury room. Only the prosecuting attorney was allowed inside.

A half hour later, Juney's face told the story. Jim Bob stood and walked over to her; we all followed in his wake.

"How did it go?" he asked.

She shook her head. "Not well, I don't think." She gulped in air. "He threw me a couple of times, and I think I sounded pretty stupid." She shook her head again. "Not good," she said.

We took our seats back in the hall, Vera and I on either side of Juney, holding her hands. Willis sat next to Jim Bob; we all, I'm sure, had rather dejected looks on our faces.

After forty-five more minutes, the prosecuting attorney came out and Jim Bob got up to speak with him. They went into another room; five minutes later, Jim Bob came out and reached for Juney.

"Outside," he said.

"But—" Vera started.

"Not a word until we're out of the courthouse, please," Jim Bob said.

Once in the parking lot of the courthouse, Jim Bob said, "They've indicted you for manslaughter, which is a second-degree felony. It carries two to twenty years and a $10,000 fine."

"Oh, God," Juney said, falling up against a parked car. Vera and I grabbed her, trying to hold her upright.

"I think I could plea it down to criminally negligent homicide, which is only six months to two years," Jim Bob said.

"But I didn't do it!" Juney cried.

Jim Bob nodded his head. "Then we'll go to court and plead innocent, Mrs. Harrell. It's your call."

"I *am* innocent!" Juney said.

Jim Bob patted her arm. "Then that's what we'll

do, my dear. And don't worry. I'm very good at what I do."

Juney nodded and started for the minivan. I shook Jim Bob's hand and thanked him, then followed Juney.

There would be no joy in Mudville tonight.

Trial was to start in two weeks. For three days, Juney sat on the couch and stared at soap operas, barely able to play with her son. She didn't eat, and by the pacing I heard at all hours of the night, I doubted that she slept. Jesse kept his nose to the grindstone, trying to stay out of Juney's way. Now wasn't the time for flirtation, and even he sensed that. I won't mention that he actually got more work on our construction done during this time, because that would appear crass.

I tried to keep myself from feeling Juney's fear. I tried to keep myself out of her shoes. I tried not to think, *There but for the grace of God . . .* But it was impossible.

The fear of incarceration. I'd been jailed for a period of several hours the year before, but I knew while I was in there that it was a very temporary situation.

The thought of going through what Juney was about to undergo—the hearings, the trial, the verdict—the horrible possibility of being sent to prison—left me gasping for air. Two to twenty years inside a prison, eating institutional food, wearing institutional clothing, trying not to be noticed, not to be hurt; hoping against hope that maybe this Saturday you'll get a visitor.

I don't know about Juney, but I consumed a lot of Maalox the days after the grand jury's decision.

The grand jury had met on Tuesday; on Friday I couldn't stand it any longer and drove into Codderville to have a little talk with Elena Luna at the Codderville PD.

Luna and I get along fine—when she's not involved in a case I have an interest in. When that happens, she acts as if I have no right whatsoever to *be* interested. *Come on,* I thought, *this is family! She can't deny me that!*

Of course she could, this was Luna we were talking about. But I went to the PD anyway.

Luna was sitting at her desk in the bull pen of the police station. We're not a large area, and we don't have a lot of cops; eight patrol officers, three detectives, some civilian personnel, and a couple of bureaucrats. Luna's desk was at the back of the bull pen, grouped with the desks of the other detectives. Hers was made distinctive by the ivy plant.

She was on the computer and the phone simultaneously as I walked up and sat in the visitor's/prisoner's chair next to her desk. She cast me one look, then turned her shoulder to me, effectively blocking my view of the computer screen. Like I cared what was on her computer screen.

I sat there patiently for what felt like an hour, but was actually only half that, before she hung up the phone and blackened the screen to her computer.

"What?" she said, barely glancing my way.

"We need to talk," I said.

She sighed, looking down at papers on her desk in a vain attempt to ignore me. "About what?"

"The Trish Glancy case."

"Go away," she said.

"I know who killed Trish," I said.

Finally, Luna looked at me. "So do I," she said. "Your sister-in-law."

"The evidence against Juney is purely circumstantial, and you know it."

"And you have hard proof against someone else?"

I decided a flanking maneuver was in order. "What do you know about Mona Glancy?" I asked.

Luna raised an eyebrow. "Wife of Edgar, stepmother of Trish, former office manager of Glancy Industries, femme fatale of the Black Cat Country Club, likes Mai Tais. Anything else?"

"A few things," I said, and smiled sweetly. "She told me—in front of a witness—that Trish Glancy never used the telephone because she was afraid of rays from outer space or something. That was a lie. Trish called several of her old high-school pals on a regularly annoying basis. Mona also said that a particular vintage motorcycle seen outside her home was there on a trial run for her husband. That was a lie. That very particular motorcycle belongs to one Tiny Malone, an outlaw biker from Sutter-Free who, by his own admission, came into a great deal of money from a person he described as 'an old broad.' It later came to my attention—and that of another witness—that Tiny Malone and Mona Glancy were having an elicit and rather kinky affair."

I took a deep breath and looked at Luna.

Again, the eyebrow came up. "Is that it?" she asked after a moment's silence.

Okay, I was going to have to spell it out for her.

"All right, look," I said. "Mona was having an affair in her home with Tiny, right? Trish was calling repeatedly begging to come home. Mona didn't want Trish at home cramping her style—"

Luna actually laughed. "So she killed her?"

"Of course not," I said. "She hired Tiny to do it."

Luna resumed studying the papers on her desk. "Bye," she said.

"Look, I've been right before! Admit it!"

"A couple of times. More often than that, though, you're wrong," she said, not looking up from her desk.

"So there's at least a fifty-fifty chance I'm right!"

Luna sighed again and put down her pen. She looked at me and slowly crossed her arms over her queenly chest. "Go away," she said slowly and succinctly. "Go away now before I have you arrested."

"For what?" I demanded.

"Being a pain in the ass."

"All I'm saying is that the only person you people have even looked at is Juney! Mona Glancy should be as big a suspect as Juney! Not to mention Barbara Nagel!"

Luna sighed. "I hate to ask, but who is Barbara Nagel?"

"The mother of one of Trish Glancy's high-school buds. The mother is convinced that Trish was to blame for Jimmy's drug use—which she wasn't according to Jimmy—and that the drug use led to Jimmy having AIDS—which it didn't because he didn't shoot up and, besides, he's gay—"

"You've lost me," Luna said. She stood up. "But

that's okay. I prefer being lost.'' She pointed toward the door. ''Leave.''

I stood up. ''I'm right about this, Luna. I know I am. Juney's innocent, and you will stand guilty of putting an innocent woman in jail or worse, and depriving a very young child of his mother!''

Luna stood up too. ''I'm sorry about the kid, E.J., I really am. It's not his fault his mother's gonna be in jail. Not any more than it's my boys' fault about their daddy. Just do what I do—tell the kid what a great mom he's got, take him to visit her, and prepare him for the day she gets out. That's what we do.''

I shook my head. ''Luna, she didn't do it.''

She sat down and went back to staring at the papers on her desk.

I turned and stormed toward the side door. I heard the front door open and glanced over to see who it was.

Liz Jones was walking into the Codderville police station. She didn't see me. I stopped, ready to tell her not to waste her breath—the powers that be were too pigheaded to listen—when she marched up to the counter that divided the visitors' area from the bull pen and asked the clerk on duty, ''May I speak to whoever is in charge of the Patricia Glancy case?''

The clerk turned toward Luna, and said, ''Elena? For you.''

Luna threw down her pen and got reluctantly to her feet, walking over to the counter. She saw me standing by the door and scowled, then ignored me.

''Yes, ma'am?'' she said to Liz.

''Are you the detective in charge of the Trish Glancy case?''

"I'm the liaison with the county sheriff's department. Can I help you?"

"I have information concerning the case," Liz said.

Luna sighed. "Yes, ma'am, and what would that be?"

Liz took a deep breath, and said, "Well, you see, it was an accident." Liz swallowed. "I didn't mean to kill her."

I was dumbfounded. No way. There was absolutely no way Liz Jones had killed Trish—accident or no accident.

Then it hit me: Mona had something on Liz. She was blackmailing her into confessing to Mona's crime. But Liz was an open book. What could Mona have on her that could force her to confess to a crime she didn't commit? Maybe one of the kids. Liz had the best kids I'd ever seen, but even very good ones sometimes do something stupid.

That had to be it. Liz would do anything for one of her kids.

I hurried up to the counter. "Liz, what the hell are you doing?" I asked.

Her face reddened when she saw me. "Go away, E.J. I have to do this."

"What has Mona got on you?" I demanded.

"Pugh!" Luna said. "Leave."

"I'm not leaving until I get some answers—"

Luna walked around the front of the counter and took Liz by the arm, then said to a passing patrol officer, "Throw this lady out," indicating me with a nod of her head.

The officer was a young man, small, scrawny; if it hadn't been for the gun on his hip, I could have taken him. Instead I let him push me out the door.

I drove back to the house wondering what the hell was going on.

The powers that be released Juney from all charges and a sentencing hearing was coming up in less than a week for Liz Jones. I intended to be there.

I called Liz's house on numerous occasions, but only got the answering machine. No messages I left were ever returned.

On Monday, two days before Liz's hearing, some good things finally began to happen. The plumbers and the electricians, under the watchful eye of Jesse Maynard, finished their work, and the flooring people were on their way. The painting had been done late at night by one of Jesse's men, and another had already built the bookcases in the master bedroom. Even the skylight was in the new master bath. For the first time, I was actually getting excited about the whole thing.

Juney had borrowed the van, and I was baby-sitting Garth, along with my own kids, when she came in the back door, tossing a teasing, flirtatious remark over her shoulder to Jesse, who beamed from ear to ear.

"Guess who you're looking at?" she asked me, standing in the doorway, arms akimbo, a wide smile on her face.

"I give up," I said. "Who?"

"Does the phrase 'Attention Kmart shoppers' mean anything to you?" she asked, still grinning.

"What?" I asked, grinning back.

"You're looking at Kmart's newest stocker. And if I'm really good, and learn fast, I'll be promoted to checker in no time flat!"

I hugged her. "Congratulations! That's great!"

Things were definitely looking up; that is, until the flooring guys got there.

We'd ordered a lovely off-white berber carpet for our bedroom; the carpet layers showed up with a royal purple plush.

And so it goes.

On Wednesday, I put on a dress, left all the kids with Vera, and went to the courthouse.

Other than lawyers, the judge, and courtroom personnel, I was the only person in the room where Liz's sentencing was taking place who didn't have a Jones in his or her name somewhere.

Liz, her husband Leonard, all five of her children and several spouses, including State Representative Garrison McLean, Connie's husband, were all in attendance.

Liz and her attorney were standing.

The judge said, "Elizabeth Jones, you have been charged with involuntary manslaughter. How do you plead?"

With a clear voice, Liz said, "Guilty, Your Honor."

Sometimes I'm not sure where the stuff comes from. I'm usually a rather upright citizen. I rarely yell "fire" in a crowded theater, I generally pay for everything I take out of a store, and I almost always stop when a policeman attempts to pull me over.

But sometimes—sometimes it just rises like cream to the top of a milk bottle. I can't suppress the inner child, the old radical, whatever it is that made me stand up and say, "Your Honor, she's lying. She didn't do this."

A whole bunch of Jones faces turned and glared at me. With one exception.

I had been right. And I had been wrong. As is so often the case. I knew who had killed Trish Glancy, and I was fairly sure I knew why.

I didn't drive home. I didn't drive to Vera's house to pick up my kids. I called Vera on my cell phone and told her I'd be a little late. She didn't seem to mind. I sat in the parking lot of the courthouse wondering what to do now. The judge, of course, had basically ignored me, except for the big burly bailiff he'd sent to escort me out of the courtroom.

I sat in the parking lot, wondering Liz's fate. Suspended sentence? Community service? Or a couple of years at the women's unit of Huntsville State Prison? Liz would probably get a suspended sentence. Of course, there was always the possibility the Glancys would sue.

She had made a decision. Who was I to say she couldn't? Who was I to say, "The truth will out"? But I couldn't leave it alone.

I started the car and drove out of town, heading out to the country.

He didn't see my van when he pulled into the long drive and let his wife off. She kissed him, took the baby out of the car seat, and headed into the house. He drove off, heading back to his office.

I got out of the minivan and met her on the porch. She looked at me. She didn't appear surprised.

"Coffee?" she asked.

I nodded and followed her inside.

Connie sat Ethan down in the middle of the great-room floor, where he began playing with his scattered toys. She went into the kitchen and started coffee brewing.

"You know," she said.

"Some of it," I said.

She nodded her head.

"How could you let your mom do this?" I asked.

Connie laughed bitterly. "You try going against a Jones family caucus. I didn't exactly have a majority vote on my side."

"Does your husband know?" I asked.

Connie shook her head. "None of the spouses know. Not even Daddy. It was just Mom and us kids. She had them all on her side. She must have been doing a lot of telephoning."

I sat down at the table and looked at the baby happily gnawing on the furniture. "It was Ethan, right? She wanted Ethan?"

Connie sat down across from me. "It happened like with Cindy. I ran into Trish at the supermarket. She was in awe of Ethan. Kept touching him." She shuddered. "It was awful, but I didn't want her to. She'd been my best friend for a long time, but the thought of those dirty fingers touching Ethan just made me sick."

I nodded. I thought I could understand; maybe not condone, but understand.

"She got our number somehow and started calling. She kept saying Ethan was hers. That I had her baby. It just got worse and worse. We had the number changed. Then she started driving by the house. She'd never get out of the car, but I'd see her out there, staring at the house."

Tears splashed down Connie's face. "That day we—Ethan and I—had gone to Mom's. We were coming back, and I knew I had to drive to Austin the next day, so I stopped at the gas station to fill up. I left Ethan in the car while I went inside to pay." Her hands were shaking as she wiped the tears from her eyes. "When I came out Trish was moving him into her car. I started yelling at her but she just jumped in her car and took off. I could hear Ethan crying—"

I patted her hand. "Connie—" I started.

"No," she said, pushing my hand away. "Let me do this. Let me get it out." She took a deep breath. "I followed her in my car. She drove out to the country, down by the river. She got out of the car and carried Ethan into the trees with her. He was still crying. I stopped the car and jumped out and followed her. She led me to the clearing where her little house was." She shook her head. "It was all so pathetic, but all I could think about was my baby. She was holding him so tightly, and he was crying so hard! She told me to go away. She said Ethan was hers, and if I didn't leave her alone, she'd jump with him into the river. She was crazy. She would have done it. She turned and started running for the river. I saw a tree limb on the ground and I picked it up and swung it. She fell and so did Ethan. I picked him up and started running back to the car with him, but she grabbed me, and I just started hitting her—hitting her where I'd already hit her in the head. Just beating on the bloody mess I'd already made.'' Connie shivered. ''She stopped. She fell down. And I ran. I got Ethan into the car, and I just drove off. I didn't know if she was dead,'' Connie said. ''I didn't know if she was alive either. I didn't really care at that point.''

I sighed. I should have seen it long before this. Trish's irrational interest in Juney's picture of Garth, the phone calls to Cindy Belton, saying, ''You have too many.'' Obviously she thought Cindy should give her one of her children. And the calls to Connie. All three women—Juney, Connie, and Cindy—had one thing in common—they were all mothers. Trish had nothing but her crooked little house in the woods. And maybe that's exactly what she was doing out there—playing house. And she needed a doll. A big, living doll to finish her fantasy.

''Has your mother known all along?'' I asked, wondering how badly Liz had played me.

Connie shook her head. ''No. I didn't tell her until your sister-in-law was indicted. I'm sorry, E.J. I shouldn't have let it get that far. But when they indicted her, I knew it had to stop. I went to Mom and told her the story, just as I told it to you. Then she started her phone calls.''

I was grateful Liz hadn't been in on it from the beginning—grateful that my friend had not played me for a fool. Instead, as soon as Connie told her what she had done, Liz, in typical Liz-fashion, had taken over, claiming the crime as her own to save her child. That it had been Connie and not Liz who should have been confessing had come clear to me the minute I saw the two of them in the courtroom. Liz was a woman who would do anything for her children. And she had.

''What was the sentence the judge gave your mother?'' I asked.

''Five years' probation, plus two years of community service. He said she could just continue the work she's already doing—you know, at the Hospice, and the hospital, and the Battered Women's Center.''

''What about Edgar Glancy? Doesn't he have a right to know the truth?'' I asked.

''Mom told him the story exactly the way it happened, but that it was her in the car instead of me.''

''Why, Connie? Why is she doing this?''

Connie shrugged. ''They all said it would be easier on her than on me. That because of my age and Garrison's politics, I might get more of a sentence. And that I needed to be home for Ethan.'' Connie started crying, sobbing. ''I let them talk me into it, E.J.! And it will always be there! I let my mother take the blame for something I did, and I'll always know that. We all will.''

I stood up and went to her putting my arms around her. ''I know a really good lawyer,'' I said.

Seventeen

August came, and with it Brenna's departure for Northwestern. We decided to fix the van and drive her there, so Juney stayed with all the kids while Willis, Vera, and I drove Brenna north.

We stayed at a nice hotel in Chicago, saw a Cubs game, went to a comedy club, listened to jazz at another club, and shopped at Marshall Field's. Then we drove to Northwestern University, and found Brenna's dorm. The dorm mother was what you'd expect, but seemed kind. I worried how Brenna would be treated once we weren't around to protect her.

Leaving her there was the hardest thing I've done since burying Terry and Roy Lester, Bessie's birth parents. Brenna had only been in our lives for a little over a year, yet I cried from Illinois to Kansas and halfway into Oklahoma. What was I going to do when it was Graham, or Megan, or Bessie?

Probably the same, I thought. It's not how long you've had a child in your life, it's how much of your heart you've given her or him. And Brenna McGraw had a great big chunk of mine, and always would.

Six weeks after Juney was released of all charges, I received a check for $24,814.97. This was my $25,000 bail, less fees for this and that. It could have been worse. With that, the addition on the house was finished. The master bedroom had a leak in the roof, but Jesse was working on getting that fixed, and there was the leak around the skylight in the bathroom, but it was all going to be okay eventually. The Jacuzzi didn't work in the sunken tub and the hot-water faucet in the separate shower stall was impossible to turn without a pair of pliers. We did get the off-white berber carpeting we'd ordered for the master suite, but had gone ahead and accepted the plank-wood floor they'd installed instead of the parquet we'd ordered for the family room. Actually, I think I liked it better.

The windows in the family room are an off size, and it's going to cost a mint to have blinds specially made, but then, who's going to be looking in our backyard anyway? Right? The window seat in the master bedroom caved in the first time I sat on it, but Jesse said that's fixable, and when the kids lay a ball down in the family room, it has a tendency to wander to the far left corner.

But, all in all, it's not bad. It could have been worse. We could still be under construction.

Edgar Glancy filed for divorce from Mona. It finally came out that Trish had been calling Mona repeatedly, begging to come home, and that Mona had been putting her off. I don't know if Edgar ever found out about Tiny, but that Mona knew where the daughter he had been searching for was—and refused to tell him—was enough for him to call a lawyer—and to invoke all the clauses in the prenup.

Connie did call Jim Bob Honeywell, and Jim Bob was with her when she told her husband the truth. Garrison McLean may have been a politician, but maybe he's too honest to go much further than state representative anyway; he called his mother-in-law and told her that Connie would be turning herself in.

With Edgar Glancy's influence, Connie's sentence was almost as minor as her mother's had been: two years of jail time, to be served on alternate weekends, and two years of community service, to be served concurrently. Like her mother, Connie was already heavily into volunteering, so that part of the sentence was easy to comply with.

I ran into Liz at church about two weeks after Connie's sentencing. She asked if she could speak to me outside after the service.

Willis took the kids to the van, and Liz and I met in the shade of a large oak on the church grounds.

"Hi," I said, walking up to where she stood, leaning against the tree.

She smiled slightly. "Hi," she said.

"How's Connie?" I asked.

Liz's face tightened. "This is her weekend in jail."

I nodded; what could I say?

Liz smiled. "She's browbeaten the county into organizing a women's intramural basketball team. The men's jail has one, but the women's doesn't. So now they do." She shrugged. "She's the captain."

"That's great," I said. "Leave it to Connie—"

"E.J. I have to say this." Liz sighed heavily.

"Yes?"

"I can't be your friend anymore. I can't stand even to see you. I know it's not fair, but it makes me angry every time I look at you. I know you did what you thought you had to do, and I know the final decision was Connie's, but she's my daughter. You're not. I have to blame you."

I couldn't answer her, tears caught in my throat. I nodded in response.

"We're changing churches. Actually, we already have. I just came here today to see you; to explain. We had everything taken care of, you didn't need to—"

"Connie was hurting, Liz. She had to tell the truth. She couldn't let you take the blame for something she did."

Liz shook her head. "It was really none of your business, E.J."

I nodded. "Yeah, you're probably right."

"Goodbye," Liz said, and turned and left me standing under the tree.

It's hard to lose a friend. Liz wasn't the first, and she probably wouldn't be the last—but it was hard. Very, very hard.

I rested my head against the tree and let the tears come. Then I dried my eyes and walked to the van to join my family.

I saw Connie briefly in September. We both sat at the back of the church at Jimmy Nagel's funeral, both of us trying to stay out of Barbara Nagel's sight. He'd fought a valiant fight, but he'd lost. Personally, I don't think I'll ever drive by a McDonald's again without thinking of him.

Connie and I held hands and shared Kleenex through the ceremony, then rode together to the cemetery for the burial. We didn't say much going over; talked about Jimmy, the weather, which was hot and muggy, and Ethan.

On the way back to the church where we'd left Connie's car, she said, "I'm so sorry my mother reacted the way she did, E.J."

I nodded. "It was her call, Connie. Actually, I understand how she feels. If it had been my child, I'm not sure that I would have reacted differently."

"It's not fair—" Connie started.

I smiled at her. "Nobody said life's supposed to be fair, Connie. I figured that out a long time ago. After all this, you should know it, too."

She nodded. "I hate to be the cause of you and Mom not being friends anymore—"

"You're not," I said, patting her hand as I pulled up next to her car. "It was my doing. But Connie, you've got to know—even after what's happened between your mother and me—I'd do it again in a heartbeat."

She reached across the space between the seats and hugged me, then jumped out of the van. That was the last time I saw Connie.

* * *

By Thanksgiving, things were going well. Brenna was on her way home from Northwestern for the holiday, most of the minor problems with the new construction were fixed (balls will always roll, but that's a small price to pay for room—blessed room).

Juney and Garth had gotten a small apartment in Codderville, within walking distance of Vera's, but since Brenna had loaned Juney her old clunker station wagon while she was up north, walking was something Juney and Garth didn't have to do. She was doing well at Kmart and had gotten the promised promotion to checker and was making an almost decent wage.

Willis and I now shared the beautiful new master bedroom on the ground floor; the girls had taken over the old upstairs master bedroom, and we'd moved Graham into the girls' old room, which was much larger than his former room. His old room was now my office, and my closet under the stairs was back to being just that—a closet.

Sometimes, when the kids and Willis are gone, I wander around my great big beautiful house, and think, "You know, maybe Willis was right." Of course, I've never told him this, and I'm begging that you don't either. You know how he gets.

Thanksgiving came and Brenna was staying at Vera's. The two drove up in Vera's ancient Valiant and honked the horn. I sent the kids out to bring in Vera's offerings: three pies, the giblet gravy I refuse to make because I think it's yucky, and Vera's infamous green-bean casserole.

Everybody hugged Brenna and she started telling

stories about the wonders of college life. The kids were glued to her every word.

We were supposed to eat at three o'clock. At three-fifteen, Juney and Garth still had not shown up. I called her apartment and got a recording, saying the phone was no longer in service.

I hung up and looked at Vera, who was busy at my stove checking the contents of all my pans to see if they were good enough. "Has Juney been having trouble paying her bills?" I asked.

Vera was sniffing my stuffing and making a face. "Who knows with that girl? She never does what I tell her to do. I said pay your bills first, then you buy frou-frous for the apartment! But will she listen to me? Of course not!"

"Her phone's been disconnected," I said.

Vera closed the oven door and turned to glare at me, arms on her hips. "And that old heap of hers probably isn't running and she hasn't got any way to call us! That girl! She'd lose her head if it wasn't attached."

"Well, I guess I should go pick her up," I said, taking a quick peek at the turkey.

"Let's just turn all this off and go. And I plan on giving her a piece of my mind, too! If she'd come over in time, she and Garth coulda ridden with me and Brenna."

We turned off the burners, and I threw a bag of popcorn at the kids who were screaming about imminent starvation, and Vera and I took the minivan into Codderville.

Juney had rented a one-bedroom apartment in a small fourplex. The door was open when we got there. The rented furniture was all there, but nothing else was. All Juney's little frou-frous, as Vera put it, all Garth's toys and clothes. Everything was gone. The only thing left that didn't belong to the landlord was a white envelope on the kitchen counter addressed to me.

I picked it up and tore it open. Inside was a handwritten note.

Dear E.J.,

I'm real sorry to do this this way, but I knew if I told y'all I was leaving, you'd find some way of talking me out of it. I know I'm wrong for doing it this way, but Vera would have a conniption and never let me go. Or let Garth go, anyway. Me, I know she can do without. Things aren't working out between Jesse and me, and I've decided I've spent too many years relying on a man—any man. I have to stand on my own two feet and do things my way—not Vera's way, not Jesse's way. My way. My manager at Kmart got me on with another store back in Houston. So we're going back there. It's mostly home anyway. My little Laurel is there, and maybe I can get to see her some. I miss her something awful. I'll be back. I promise. Please tell Brenna I'm just borrowing her car, and I'll get it back to her at Christmas, if y'all would like me to visit. Me and Garth sure would like that—and maybe we can bring Laurel with us. I'll call when I get a phone and let you know where we are. Thanks for everything.

If it hadn't been for you, E.J., I'd probably be wearing stripes—or whatever the latest prison fashion is! Ha! Ha!

Love,
Juney

I read the note out loud. By the time I'd finished, Vera was standing at the window, looking out at the gray day beyond.

"Vera," I started, walking up behind her.

"I try to be a good Christian woman, E.J.," she said, her voice catching, "but sometimes I'm just an old fool."

I put my arms around her, resting my chin on her head. "You're not an old fool, Vera. You've got a lot of love to give, and I'm glad my family's here to get it. Juney's just too young to know how to take it. She'll learn."

"Am I ever gonna see my boy again?" she asked.

"If it harelips Texas," I said. "And maybe you'll get a new granddaughter to boot. Now," I said, grabbing her arm, "we've got a lot of hungry mouths to feed and it is, by God, Thanksgiving."

"What have I got to be thankful for?" she asked.

"Willis, Graham, Megan, Bessie, Brenna. Hell, Vera, even me."

She laughed. "Well, at least you've still got your sense of humor," she said.

I shook my head, and we headed to the van.